Whimsy and Sterling

REBECCA MACCEILE

FOR C.S.

Thank you for the magic. I wish I would have recognized it earlier and been able to follow up with our lunch date. Live and learn.

All the best,
Becca

CONTENTS

1 FORGED IN FLAME

The sun slowly began to peek over the horizon as Paul shuffled quietly down the street. He had been making the same journey for nearly sixty years: three short city blocks from his well kept brownstone to his small jewelry shop. Paul sighed as he dug into the left pocket of his well worn khaki slacks, searching blindly for his keys. After several moments he produced a large silver keychain.

"There you are, old friend." He mumbled to his reflection, which shone back brightly in the orange hue of the morning sun.

He paused for a moment. He carefully studied himself in the reflection as he read the small inscription: Wilson's Jewelry Emporium Est. July 1955. He remembered the day that he hammered those words gingerly into the soft sterling. It felt like no time had passed at all. He ran his finger over the letters who's edges had softened with time and care; then, he inserted the small brass key into the lock and opened the heavy wooden-framed door.

Cynthia, his daughter, had always lectured him about maintaining the original door to his business. While he had upgraded the windows with new security measures, he was somewhat sentimental about the door. Unbeknownst to Cynthia, Paul and his late wife Wanda had inscribed their initials quietly into the corner of the frame. He knew it was somewhat of a security risk, but he still felt obligated to keep it. The door creaked in protest as it closed softly behind him.

"I know, old girl. The weather is starting to turn. It hurts my old bones too." Paul spoke as he continued around to each of the small shop windows to lift the security gates and allow the morning light through. Once the gates opened and the sun shone brightly illuminating the small space, Paul set about uncovering and organizing the display cases. He was exceptionally proud of his displays. Ninety percent of the jewelry in his shop he crafted himself. Being a silversmith wasn't just a way to make a living. Paul put time and soul into each of his pieces. If the customer wanted to know the story behind an item before making a purchase, Paul could tell them. He remembered each detail as if he were speaking of his children.

Of course, in today's modern society, many of his customers no longer cared about the intricacies of hand made items, and were only concerned with the bottom line. How much does it cost, and do you finance? That was all he ever seemed to discuss with his patrons lately, many of whom were sons and daughters of his very first customers. It was nice to have the loyalty of his patrons. However, Paul desperately missed the genuine interactions and sincere appreciation for his work.

After removing the covers from his stock and turning the lights on in each display case, Paul stopped to stretch his aging back. After he finished his stretch, he walked over to unlock the door and flip the sun-faded sign baring his business hours to open. He paused and looked out the window into the quiet city street. A few of his neighboring business owners were beginning to make their way in for the day. Cars began to line the limited spaces in front of the small row of shops as birds fought over small crumbs they had procured from dumpsters nearby.

Paul loved his shop and the small neighborhood boro it occupied. As if a stark reminder, his arthritic hand began to throb. He knew his days as a jeweler were slowly drawing to a close, but he wasn't ready to give up his irons just yet.

He walked behind the counter and began to set up his desk for the afternoon. The local high school would be releasing its latest graduates in the coming months, and Paul was making custom class rings. It was a service he offered since the shop first opened, but each year the number of students willing to spend the extra cost to receive a custom ring was dwindling. Out of the latest class of several hundred students, Paul was only commissioned to make twenty rings.

He opened his workbench and carefully lay his tools upon the velvet cloth, which protected them from the elements. He checked them for damage or other wear and tear. He had practiced this ritual each day for so many years it had become a habit. His tools weren't getting nearly as much use as they had been in years past, but he felt compelled to check them at the beginning of each day regardless.

As he finished setting the tools on the table, he paused to admire them. They were the only remaining friends from his youth; everyone else had passed on either from life itself or the neighborhood. Paul had his children, but he was at odds with them more often than not. They loved him and wanted the best for him in his ripe old age. Still, somewhere between teenagehood and adulthood, they had forgotten their father was capable of taking care of himself. His arthritis flared up occasionally, and he wasn't as quick on his feet, but he was still a man in command of his business and his life.

His face crumpled into a scowl at the thought of Cynthia's latest lecture, and he huffed as he rose from the small stool to don his leather apron. He carefully tied the worn straps around his waist before returning to his seat and adjusting his glasses.

Paul almost picked up his mandrel when he was interrupted as the bell above the door let out a loud jingle. A rather tall man dressed in a smart suit and cap entered the shop.

"Hello, welcome to Wilson's Jewelry Emporium. Can I help you, sir?" Paul called as he folded his glasses before sticking them into his breast pocket and rising to meet his guest.

"Yes, thank you. I'm looking for someone to make a custom pendant for my wife. Is that something you can help me with?" The gentleman asked, politely removing his cap.

"Let me see. Do you have something specific in mind?" Paul answered, honestly.

"I do. Are you familiar with the significance of the Shinto Omamori custom?" Paul's guest asked.

"No. I can't say that I am." Paul answered.

"Ah, well briefly for time's sake, I have an appointment, as part of the Shinto religion a priest often inscribes small talismans to provide luck or protection from the various Kami. Kami, being deities. I'd like to have a specific inscription made as a necklace for my wife." The gentleman explained.

Paul thought heavily.

"I'm not a priest, sir. I don't think that..." Paul began.

"Oh, yes. I know. I'm not concerned with that. Can you make the inscription?" The gentleman interrupted.

"Well, yes. It should be a simple project. I don't know if I'm entirely comfortable with it. If it has a religious significance, it should be crafted by someone who practices the religion. It's a matter of respect." Paul answered.

The gentleman smiled warmly.

"I deeply appreciate your concern. I assure you, Mr.

Wilson if you're able to manufacture the pendant for me, you are more than worthy." The gentleman insisted.

Paul looked intently at the man standing before him. He couldn't figure him out. The man was tall, with grey, almost white hair, broad shoulders, and his suit impeccably tailored. He could go anywhere to have this piece of jewelry made for his wife. He could probably afford the flight to Japan if he wanted to. Paul couldn't understand why he would seek out a small independent shop like his.

"You have an outstanding reputation, Mr. Wilson. I traveled a long way to visit you this morning. I admire your principals, and if you choose not to take my commission, I understand. Please, give me a call. I have to be going. I'll be in town until tomorrow evening." The gentleman said, producing a business card from within his jacket. "This symbol, it's Kanji representing happiness and good fortune. Please consider." The gentleman explained as he pointed to a small character printed on the reverse of his card.

Paul took the card and fumbled with his glasses. Once his glasses perched on the bridge of his nose, he peered at the card again. It read: Mr. Jack Johnson CEO.

"I'll consider it, Mr... Johnson," Paul answered.

"Thank you. I hope you will take the commission, Mr. Wilson. Have a wonderful afternoon.

I look forward to hearing from you." Mr. Johnson said with a small bow as he placed his hat back on his head and quickly walked out the door.

Paul turned to place the business card and his glasses back into his breast pocket as the bell above the door let out a bright jingle once again. He turned around, expecting to see Mr. Johnson had returned for something. Instead, he met with only the shop and his wares gleaming brilliantly in the mid-morning sun.

"Hello?" Paul called.

He was met instead with another jingle of the doorbell and a quiet draft of cool air.

"Odd," Paul mumbled to himself as he sat down to his workbench and returned to his project.

The day wore on with no additional foot traffic. Paul was able to finish his commissioned class rings and sit down to design the pendant for Mr. Johnson. He began with a simple square and decided that he would chisel the design by hand. These days Paul often opted for his electric burr to facilitate quick and easy engraving. However, for Mr. Johnson, he knew the piece needed the loving attention that only hand engraving could offer. Paul checked the measurements of his sketch twice more before rising from his workbench and heading to the stockroom. He carefully selected a medium length silver box chain and small blank square pendant that he had been saving for the holiday season.

"I guess these will do. I don't believe I'll have Marry and Babbette's custom order this year." Paul muttered to himself as he held the pendant and chain next to one another, comparing the luster and color of the two. When he was satisfied that he found a match, he returned to his workbench and laid them out side by side.

Leaving his workbench, he made his way to the front door and gently flipped the sign to display the "closed" script before throwing the lock and turning out the lights in each display case. He quietly returned each velvet cover to their proper place. Then he stretched his back once again before taking a seat at the bench and reaching into his pocket. He pulled out Mr. Johnson's business card. He lay it on his workbench and pulled out his glasses. Once he could adequately read the number, he picked up the cordless telephone and dialed.

The line buzzed several times before the classic ring tone filled Paul's ear. He waited as it rang several times until a chipper female voice called: "Hello, Mr. Johnson's Office, how may I help you?"

"Yes, hello. It's Paul Wilson. I just wanted to let Mr. Johnson know that I will be happy to fulfill his commissioned order. I should have it ready within the week. If he would like to discuss the cost, he can reach me at 342-0908 between the hours of 9 am-7 pm." Paul explained quickly but clearly.

"Oh, that's wonderful. Mr. Johnson will be pleased to hear that. What was the number again?" The cheerful receptionist asked as she shuffled paper around and clicked a pen.

"342-0908," Paul repeated.

"Thank you, Mr. Wilson. I'll relay the message to him as soon as possible."

"Thank you… I'm sorry I didn't catch your name?" Paul asked, but before he could finish his question, the line went dead.

"Well, I guess that's that then." Paul huffed as he returned the phone to its cradle and began to gather his things and head home for the evening. He considered storing the chain and new pendant overnight but instead opted to leave them on his workbench. Aside from Mr. Johnson, no one had even window shopped at the store. There was no reason to think anyone would even notice the small shop after hours.

Paul quietly returned his tools to their drawers, slipped on his coat, and headed for the door. Before he could reach the door, a cold wind blew from behind him, voraciously ringing the doorbell, and launching the old door wide open.

"What on Earth?" Paul exclaimed as he quickly grabbed the large wooden door to prevent it from breaking the hinges. As soon as his foot crossed the threshold, the wind stopped. "Now you hold on just a minute there… whatever you are. Don't show up and make a mess of my shop, or I'll call Mr. Johnson back right now and cancel the order," Paul scolded, gesturing broadly at the emptiness around him.

Paul met an eerie silence in return; then, he quietly

closed the door and engaged the lock.

"I must be tired. I need to get home and lie down. Goodnight, old girl." Paul whispered as he patted the door handle as if he were saying goodbye to an old friend before heading down the street toward home.

The next morning Paul shuffled into the shop as usual ready to begin his day the same way that he started his days for the past sixty-four years. He opened the door carefully, paused to admire the initials carved into the frame, and listened to the slow squeak of tired hinges as the door closed behind him. Paul reached for the lightswitch entirely out of habit while simultaneously clicking the lock on the door behind him. As the old florescent lights flickered to life and his eyes adjusted, he was in shock.

"What in the world?" He gasped.

The shop was immaculate, and each display case was already open for the business day. Each piece filling the display was sparkling with a freshly polished gleam that Paul hadn't seen in ages. Concerned at this strange turn of events, Paul immediately rushed to the backroom to check his inventory. At first glance, it didn't appear that anything was missing from the cases in the front room. He couldn't understand who or what would gain access to the shop solely to polish his wares.

Much to Paul's relief, he found the safe, securely locked, and what little cash he kept on hand in the change fund balanced. He relaxed as he set about taking a thorough inventory of the front room display. Each piece was where he left it; the only difference was the polish and missing dust covers.

"Huh. Well, whatever you are, thank you. I don't know why you did that for me, but I did need to clean up the inventory. Where did you put my dust covers?" Paul spoke, looking out into the empty shop.

Suddenly, a loud thump sounded behind him. He slowly

turned around, expecting to see an intruder lurch at him, but instead saw the dust covers strewn across the floor. It looked like they had been folded on his bench and fallen.

At that, Paul laughed.

"Alright. You've had your fun, Mr. Johnson. Who's here? Where have you been hiding?" Paul called as he bent down to retrieve the dust covers and return them to their proper home.

He received only silence and a gentle breeze brushing past his face.

"I admit those are some pretty fancy tricks, but I'm too old to fall for magic, Mr. Johnson," Paul mumbled.

He shook his head with a chuckle as he continued the necessary chores to open the shop for the business day.

Soon he flipped the sign to display the faded open script and made his way to the workbench. He placed his tools within reach, tied his apron, donned his glasses, and sat down to work. The chain and pendant were where he left them the night before. Considering the other events of the morning, he was surprised to find them undisturbed. He carefully placed the pendant into the desktop vice and made sure it was secure before digging out Mr. Johnson's card with the symbol he requested.

Paul traced the design with meticulous precision into a rubber stamp. He carefully pressed the stamp into the ink pad and onto the pendant. When Paul was satisfied that the design was centered and symmetrical, Paul carefully selected the necessary scorper and pressed it into the soft sterling silver. After the rough outline began to show through, he replaced the scorper with a spit stick and brought the design to life.

Paul spent the previous evening researching various techniques to recreate Kanji correctly. Typically, the characters were applied onto parchment or silk with careful brushstrokes. He took great care to recreate the fluid appearance of brushstrokes as he honed the design. Paul was entranced with his work. He took care to perfect each piece he created, but something about this pendant was different. Once he finished the engraving, he paused to look at his work.

Mr. Johnson hadn't been particular in what he wanted the design to look like, other than the Kanji inscribed on a necklace. Paul watched the light reflect off the fresh cut pendant and decided that it needed something else. Time would eventually tarnish the negative space. Silver was a fickle metal. It wouldn't take much for the oxidation to become noticeable, and yet he still thought the piece was missing something.

He scowled at the piece as he thought of what he could do to make the Kanji stand out against the bare metal. He thought about paint, but that seemed like a cheap short cut. He could oxidize the negative space chemically. Still, it was a risky procedure that might damage the integrity of the pendant all together.

"What do I need, huh?" Paul spoke quietly to the empty room.

As if to answer his crucible began to rattle on the shelf across the room. The flash of recognition shone over his expression. Niello, it was perfect. The process would be time-consuming, and he was certainly out of practice, but the deep black contrast was just what the pendant required. He carefully left the pendant snug in the vice as he stood up, stretched his back, and began gathering the necessary tools and ingredients for the niello.

He shuffled to and fro in his storage room, first collecting his crucible, torch, and ladle. He returned to his workbench, setting everything down in a specific arrangement, then set about firing the furnace necessary for preparing the various ingredients. Working with heat and flame was one of his favorite parts of being a silversmith. However, it was time consuming and dangerous work as his eyesight began to wane. Generally, if he required the furnace or any other molten metalwork, he would schedule a time for Cynthia to help him. This time, he made an exception.

The furnace roared to life as he ignited the burner and made sure to check the temperature. He glanced at his watch. He noted the time the furnace should be at the proper temperature and continued back to the storeroom to collect the rest of his materials. A few moments later, he set the necessary ingredients down next to the crucible as he fetched his tongs and double-checked the temperature of the furnace.

He carefully secured the delicate crucible into place with the tongs, grabbed his well-worn fireproof gloves, and set to work. He added the proper ingredients to the crucible as it reached temperature and began to glow red hot. The metal sparked and hissed as it began to melt. Paul had forgotten how much it thrilled him to watch something so substantial, yet so delicate melt into a puddle. He left the crucible and his mixture to sit as he prepared the second half of the niello equation.

Using his third-hand stand, he set up the steel melting ladle above the small flame of his torch. He carefully flipped on the overhead exhaust hood to draw the fumes out, then set to work melting and mixing the lead and sulfur necessary to bond the niello mixture to the sterling. It was a quick process that resulted in a burst of smoke and hiss of flames. Soon, the two combinations were ready to be joined into one furious fire.

The metal seemed to dance as he combined the mixtures and stirred them with a steel stirring rod. Where the lead and other metal had been glowing with liquid heat as individuals, everything immediately became a dark black bubbling cauldron as soon as the two were mixed.

"Ha! I've still got it." Paul called proudly to himself, watching the metals mix and meld to the proper consistency.

He continued to stir, ensuring the proper mixture before he completed the smelting process by cooling the niello in a flux bath of ammonium chloride. As soon as the molten metal hit the bath, it began to break into small pieces as if it had been shocked. Paul carefully collected the granules and added them to his pestle, where he ground them into a thin paste.

When the paste was complete, Paul began to apply the niello around the delicate Kanji inside the charm. He took the smallest spatula in his tool kit and carefully scooped the mixture from the cauldron and took ample time to place it correctly within the delicate lines.

As he inspected his finished product, he flipped on the small heat lamp near his workbench and lay the newly formed piece under the heat to dry. He loved the way the niello's deep blackness seemed to make the sterling pop out from the background. It was what he envisioned when he started the project, and Paul swelled with pride as he watched the finished product jump from his imagination and into reality.

Paul busied himself, cleaning and storing his equipment. The pendant would need time to dry before he could complete the process. He made a bit extra niello and would need to save it as well as making sure his crucible was clean and prepared for the next time he might need it. The cleaning process was tedious, but he enjoyed it. His father had always told him that cleanliness was next to godliness. The senior Wilson also worked hard to instill the love of order and attention to detail that would serve Paul well later in life.

Of course, as a child, Paul was resistant to follow his father's advice. He felt compelled to blaze his trail as he left home a headstrong, independent teenager. As the years wore on, eventually, Paul was able to see the wisdom in his father's words and applied them to his profession. Now, at the ripe old age of eighty-one, Paul couldn't imagine doing things any other way. Everything had a place, and everything was in its place as long as Paul had something to say about it.

Once his tools were clean and properly stored away, Paul checked on the pendant. It was ready for firing. This process would require something a bit different than a furnace or a torch. Paul carefully picked up the jewelry and carried it across the shop to the small kiln he kept primarily for any pieces involving niello. The kiln was the product of neglect in recent years.

"Oh my. I guess it's been a bit longer than I thought." Paul coughed as he brushed a thin layer of dust from the outside of the kiln and its controls. "Old girl, don't burn down the house."

Paul turned around to find a suitable firebrick to support the pendant during the firing process, and when he turned back to the kiln, he met a swirl of dust and ash.

"Hey! Hey now, that's enough!" Paul called, waving his free hand in front of his face to disperse the dust and ash sent aloft.

As quickly as it started, the dust cloud and ash settled quietly to the floor. The kiln was left immaculate in its wake.

Paul stared at the kiln, then turned around, surveying every small space where a person might be able to hide. Finding no evidence of anyone besides himself in the shop, he returned to the task at hand. Paul selected the correct temperature on the controls and lit the kiln. It wouldn't take long for the kiln to reach the proper temperature, and soon he would be able to see the fruits of his labor. He was excited at the opportunity to watch the niello set. It was one of his favorite parts of the technique. He sat the pendant and firebrick on the counter and shuffled his way back to the front of the shop. He glanced at his watch and the shadows outside the shop windows. He spent nearly the entire business day carefully working on the piece for Mr.

Johnson. Time had passed so quickly he was almost unaware of it.

"Hmm…" He muttered, again looking at his watch. "I think I have time to finish this part tonight. The polishing will have to wait until tomorrow."

As if the kiln could hear his thoughts, the timer sounded alerting him that the kiln was ready. He paused to listen for the sound again in complete disbelief. The kiln usually took at least half an hour to reach the proper temperature. After a few moments, the music rang through the shop.

"I'll be…" Paul gasped, returning to the kiln and double-checking the settings.

Heat radiated off of the small machine, and he could see the red glow of the filaments through the little heat resistant glass door.

"Well, whatever you are, you're kind of handy to have around. I'll be sad to see this piece go." Paul chuckled to himself as he donned his gloves, and placed the firebrick with the pendent nestled on top directly into the kiln before shutting the door.

Due to the heat of the kiln, it didn't take long before the niello began to bubble. It slowly melted into a white haze as the flux spread and evaporated from the mixture. Like a thunderstorm rolling across the horizon, the white mist soon gave way to a dull red glow, then a bright red glow, and eventually, the niello melted and set itself into the negative space left behind by Pauls's careful craftsmanship.

Paul watched every process with a growing smile across his face. He loved taking raw materials that others would find lackluster or useless and turning them into something coveted by even the most fastidious of customers. As the bubbling began to subside and the niello settled, paul removed the brick and pendent from the flames to inspect his work.

The first application was flawless, and Paul swelled with pride.

"I've still got it, Whatever You Are. Look at that. Just look at that." Paul laughed as he removed his gloves and set them aside. The pendent would have to cool overnight before it was ready for polishing.

He smiled again as he triple checked the pendent for quality, before shutting down the equipment and closing the shop for the day.

2 HAPPINESS

Jack Johnson straightened his suit coat and necktie after he stepped from his private car into the bustle of downtown foot traffic. He smiled as the bright sun filtered through the smog and refraction from the skyscrapers surrounding him. It felt good to have some natural light hit his skin, even if it was only for a moment before he disappeared into his office for the day. Jack tipped his hat. He waved his driver on before quickly walking across the wide sidewalk and greeting the doorman of his building.

"Hello, James. How are you this morning?" Jack called with a respectful tip of his hat.

"I'm well, Mr. Johnson. Thank you. How is Tabitha fairing after the loss, Sir? If I may ask." James replied as he opened the large mirrored brass door allowing Jack to enter.

"Thank you, James. She's not well at the moment, but we're hoping that she turns a corner in these next few days." Jack answered, removing his hat and placing it under his arm.

"I'm sorry to hear that, Sir. We'll keep her in our prayers, Sir." James answered with a small bow as Jack continued through the lobby and toward the large bank of elevators.

Jack paused briefly before stepping into a large elevator with a crowd of other office neighbors quietly making their way to the various floors throughout the building. At one time, Jack knew who occupied every floor and most of the employees. Yet, when his wife Tabitha fell ill several years ago, his attention to the details of who was in and out of his building had waned. Now he rode in silence with strangers that dwindled until he remained alone as the elevator doors squeaked open on the top floor.

"Goodmorning, Mr. Johnson." Becky, his receptionist, called cheerfully. "Mr. Wilson has agreed to make the jewelry for you, Sir. He said it should be ready by Friday. He called late last night, just before I left for the evening."

"Goodmorning, Becky. That's wonderful news. Thank you." Jack responded as he continued past the front desk and through the cubicles to his own private office.

He smiled and exchanged pleasantries with many of his employees. A gesture that he felt was necessary for company morale and basic human kindness. Yet he knew the majority of his workforce had no interest in him or his personal life. The majority of people he spoke to each morning were only interested in one thing, and that thing was their success. The conversations were shallow, and most of them meaningless. It drained him more and more each day, and he was relieved to reach the sanctuary of his private room.

As he closed the door and left the bustle and noise of the cubicles behind him, he breathed a sigh of relief. He then shed his coat, straightened his tie once again, and threw open the massive steel blinds to let the sunlight illuminate the room. He paused as he positioned his hands over his hips and stared out across the expanse of the city. His building wasn't the tallest or the most impressive architecturally, but he was proud of it. He gazed out into the world a few moments more before sitting down behind his large oak desk and opening several files that he had been reviewing. It was going to be a long and tedious day of meetings and paperwork. He was looking forward to the end of the day when he could leave all the facade behind and return to Tabitha's side at Mercy West.

It had been five years since her cancer diagnosis with little improvement to her condition regardless of different treatments. Making things worse for her, mentally more so than physically, they had discovered her cancer during a routine ultrasound late into her first pregnancy. She had opted to delay treatment until the baby was born, but fate had other plans. Three weeks later, their only son, Julian, was stillborn. Tabitha never recovered. She only managed to leave the hospital for a few short weeks until cancer became too much for her fragile body to fight on its own. Ever since, Jack had remained dutifully by her side each night as long as the nurses would allow him to be there.

Tabitha wasn't improving, but she wasn't declining either. It seemed like she was stuck somewhere in between life and death, grieving for the loss of her child. She had no more will to live, yet no means to die. It devastated Jack to watch his wife dance between worlds. They had access to all the financial means in the world to combat her illness, but nothing could buy her way to happiness again. At least, nothing until Jack had stumbled across the art of Shinto blessings, and significance of Kanji. It was his last hope to save his dear Tabitha when all other science and religion had failed him.

Paul had a new spring in his step as he walked down the broad iron staircase from his front door onto the sidewalk. He was excited to complete the pendant and call Mr. Johnson to deliver the news that the piece was ready. There was a slight chill in the air, but Paul could barely feel it. He was overflowing with the warmth that only came from a day of hard work and a job well done. He waved and called out to his neighbors as he passed them, each of them reacting with surprise and returning his genuine smile.

Paul usually kept to himself, however he couldn't help but share the joy that filled his heart as he made his way down the street. Soon he arrived to find the shop inventory once again, freshly polished, clean, and entirely gleaming. The doorbell clattered as he entered, and instead of a single groan, the door fell closed with a soft thump against the frame.

"Good morning to you too, Whatever You Are. It's nice to see you were busy last night." Paul laughed as he shed his light jacket, stowed it safely under his workbench, and finished the necessary chores to open the store for the business day. He was in a hurry to deliver the class rings to the highschool. Afterward, he was taking the necklace to Mr. Johnson.

He quickly gathered and boxed each ring into a snug jewelry box, then quietly into a larger cardboard box before sealing it with packing tape.

"That's done. Now, where's the beauty. I left it by the kiln, didn't I?" Paul muttered to himself as he set the box of rings underneath the front display counter and made his way across the shop to the kiln room.

Just as he expected, he found the pendent exactly where he left it the night before. It was sitting quietly on the firebrick, awaiting the final steps neccesary before delivery. For the first time since the day before, Paul was able to handle the pendant with his bare hands. The silver felt warm and somehow electric as he picked it up from its resting place. He held it up to the light to admire the reflection and the light shone brightly across the sterling surface.

"I don't know how, but you've managed to retain your luster through the fire. You don't need too much polishing to make you shine, do you now?" Paul spoke softly to the pendant.

It glistened in response as a small draft quietly flowed

through the shop.

"Oh, I guess you had something to do with that, huh?" Paul spoke to the empty room as the cool air continued to swirl around him.

The doorbell jingled softly in response, and Paul smiled as he carried the pendant back to the front of the store from the kiln room and sat down at his workbench. Once he was comfortable in his seat, he leaned over and pulled out the small polisher he had used for years. It was a little fickle in terms of performance, but mostly it was reliable enough. He'd never found another that worked as well and stubbornly refused to replace it.

He sat the polisher on his workbench, unwound the cord and plugged it in. He then carefully selected a buffing wheel, attached it, and quietly went to work. The dull hum of the rapidly spinning wheel was comforting as he applied the polishing compound to the silver and gingerly buffed it off once again.

Soon he could see his reflection in the pendant. When he was satisfied with its luster and shine, he set it aside. He gave the same meticulous care to the chain that would pair with the pendant. Once he finished with the chain, he carefully slid the chain through the pendant's bale and again paused to hold his finished project up to the fluorescent light.

The necklace was exquisite. Not only did it sparkle in the artificial light, but it also caught the small rays of sun filtering in through the shop windows and sent them bouncing around the shop.

"Perfect," Paul said with a smile, lowering the necklace back to the workbench before selecting a red velvet box for it's home. He packaged the necklace first in velvet, then again in cardboard for the journey to Mr. Johnson's office. Paul wasn't in the habit of delivering his wares to anyone aside from loyal customers these days. But something about the necklace demanded a personal touch.

Paul placed the package next to the class rings, and quietly closed up his shop. He donned his light jacket, tucked the necklace into his breast pocket, and held the box of rings securely under his arm before heading out to make his deliveries. As he was walking out the door, once again, the doorbell jingled, and a cool breeze brushed past him.

"I'll miss having you around. It was nice to have some company for a while." Paul said, throwing the lock and testing the door.

As soon as he was sure that the shop was secure, Paul tucked his keyring into his pants pocket and began the short walk toward the high school. He planned to deliver the rings first, then hail a cab and head to Johnson Tower.

Jack, lost in thought, barely even heard the phone ring, but eventually, it broke through his concentration, and he reached for the receiver to answer.

"Yes, this is Mr. Johnson." He muttered in between sips of coffee and shuffling papers around on his desk.

"Mr. Johnson, you have a visitor, Sir. Mr. Wilson? He said he has a delivery for you." Becky's shrill voice sounded through the phone.

"Mr. Wilson? I wasn't expecting him, but certainly. Send him in Becky. Thank you." Jack said as he returned the receiver to its cradle and straightened his tie.

"Hello?" Paul called as he slowly opened the large office door.

"Mr. Wilson, it's good to see you. How can I help you?" Jack answered as he stood from his desk to help Paul through the door.

"I have your order here. Normally, I don't deliver things these days, but something about this piece. Well, it's just special, Mr. Johnson. I've been honored to work on it for you." Paul answered as he pulled the small cardboard box from his breast pocket and handed it to Jack.

Jack took the box and set it on his desk as he continued

to open it. He took the lid off the cardboard box and lifted the velvet case to eye level before flipping it open. As soon as the silver hit the light, it seemed to glow.

"Mr. Wilson... This necklace is splendid." Jack exclaimed entranced by the pendant.

"It did turn out fairly well," Paul answered as his cheeks began to flush.

It didn't matter how many years he had been in business. Paul always loved to see the look on a customer's face when they were genuinely pleased with his work.

"Mr. Wilson... I can't thank you enough. This piece is stunning; it's beyond words. Please stop at the front desk on your way out. Becky will tend to your payment and cab fare." Jack instructed as he took Paul's hand in a firm handshake.

"Thank you, Mr. Johnson. It was a pleasure to work for you. If you need anything else, you know where to find me." Paul replied with a smile.

Paul turned to walk out the door and back toward the front desk stealing just one more glance at the pendant glistening in the afternoon light.

Jack carefully put the necklace back into its velvet box and quickly finished the few projects he had on his desk. He couldn't wait to deliver the necklace to Tabitha. Yes, Jack was the owner of the company, and nothing was keeping him at the office, aside from personal responsibility. He felt obligated to be at work as often as his employees. He felt like it set a good precedent and boosted company morale to see the CEO arrive at work with them, and often leave after them.

He glanced at his watch, then glanced at the small red box before closing his folder. He packed a few notable projects that he could finish at the hospital and decided to head out for the day.

"Becky," he called through the intercom. "I'm leaving a

little bit early today. Please hold my calls."

"Yes. Mr. Johnson. Of course. Is everything okay?" Becky replied.

"Yes, everything is fine. I'm just taking the afternoon off. I'll be leaving through my private elevator. Have a good evening, Becky. I'll see you tomorrow." Jack responded as he threw his suit coat over his shoulders and headed for the door.

Instead of waiting for his private car, Jack opted to hail a cab. He exited the back of the building on the opposite side of the block. He was out of practice, but soon a taxi pulled up in front of him, and he was able to climb inside.

"Where are you going?" The cab driver asked roughly.

"Mercy West, please. The South wing, if you can." Jack answered.

"Sure, but the meter is running." The driver answered, pulling out into traffic and heading in the direction of the hospital.

"Yes. I'm aware. Thank you." Jack answered, gently patting the velvet box in his coat pocket.

The ride continued in silence, for which Jack was thankful. He had too much on his mind to participate in polite conversation, and the driver seemed to be receptive to Jack's general mood. Soon they pulled into the large parking garage on the South pavilion of the hospital.

"Thank you, Sir. I won't require your services for the ride home." Jack said as he pulled several bills from his wallet to cover the fair plus a generous tip.

The driver nodded as he accepted the payment before pulling back into the flow of traffic and making his way out of the garage.

Jack started the all too familiar trek through the maze of parking and hallways in the hospital. When Tabitha began her life in the hospital, he carried a detailed map of the hospital corridors. Now, after so many years, Jack felt he knew these lonely hallways even better than he knew the rooms in his own home. He smiled and nodded toward many of the staff as he wound his way through the labyrinth until finally, he reached the proper floor.

"Hello, Gloria. Is she awake?" Jack asked as he paused at the nurses' station to inquire about Tabitha's condition.

"Hello, Mr. Johnson. She is awake. She just finished her lunch. She's having a good day today." Gloria answered with a smile. "Go on back. I'm sure she'll be thrilled to see you."

Jack delivered a broad smile as he continued down the hallway until he reached Tabitha's room. She was fortunate enough to acquire a private room, and as her tenure had been so long, the decor in the room suited her taste. The pastel floral curtains ruffled quietly in the breeze sent aloft by the hospital's HVAC. She was sitting in her bed, watching the world float by through her window, pale, gaunt, and merely a shell of the formidable woman he married so many years ago.

It made his heart hurt to see her this way. He hoped with sheer irrationality that the Omamori magic held within this charm would revive her soul so she could fight cancer ravaging her body.

"Tabitha, my love, how are you?" He called as he walked into the room and set his briefcase, hat and suit jacket onto the one sitting chair in the corner of the room.

"Jack, you're early," Tabitha answered with a smile as she turned her attention from the window toward her husband.

"Yes, I am a little bit early. I have something for you." Jack replied, sitting on the bed next to his wife and withdrawing the small box from behind his back.

Tabitha took the box and opened it.

"Jack. It's beautiful, but why?" Tabitha asked, as she gently took the necklace from it's resting place and quickly draped it around her neck.

"In Japan, the Shinto religion ascribes to the belief that

everything has a Kami, or god to look after it. These Kami can be attracted to or repelled from you with inscriptions of Kanji like this character here. It means happiness, my love. I want to see your eyes sparkle again the way that this necklace sparkles around your neck." Jack explained.

Tabitha brought her frail hand to the pendant.

"I love it, Jack. Thank you." She whispered as a cool breeze filtered through the room.

Jack wrapped his arm around his wife. He gave her a firm but gentle hug before returning to the opposite side of the room to continue his paperwork while Tabitha slept. He remained dutifully by her side until visiting hours at the hospital were over. They ate dinner together; they laughed together. If the nurses hadn't made their rounds, and the doctors didn't check various medications, Jack would have forgotten that they were in the hospital altogether. It wasn't immediate, but he could swear that her eyes seemed brighter after she woke from her nap.

Jack packed up his things as visiting hours drew to a close, kissed his beloved wife goodnight, and made his way quietly back through the labyrinth of corridors. Soon he reached the street and the car waiting for him.

"Good evening, Mr. Johnson. How is she today?" Larson, Jack's faithful driver, asked as Jack slid into the back seat.

"Hello, Larson. She's doing quite well, thank you. Could you do me a favor before we head home?" Jack replied, situating his belongings, unbuttoning his jacket, and removing his hat.

"Yes, of course, Sir. What is it?" Larson answered, checking the rearview mirror before slowly pulling into the flow of traffic.

"Could we drive through the park tonight? I haven't been through the park in ages. I'd love to see the fall colors on the leaves." Jack answered.

"Say no more, Mr. Johnson. I'd love to see the fall

colors myself. It should be a beautiful drive." Larson answered with a genuine smile before turning toward the park.

It took them about half an hour to fight evening traffic from the hospital to the park, but Jack didn't mind. He felt rejuvenated and refreshed after the beautiful evening spent with Tabitha. Maybe it was only his imagination or the last glimmer of false hope, but he thought that she looked better when he left. Perhaps she didn't look better in a physical sense. Still, she seemed to be glowing as if the spark of her existence reilluminated from a dull flicker into a full-fledged flame. The zeal that she lost after the devastation appeared to be returning, even if slowly, and it was contagious.

By the time they reached the park, the sun had set behind the tall buildings, but the park was still bustling with activity. Many of the trees were illuminated with twinkling white lights to highlight the changing of the seasons. Their colors weren't visible in all of their glory, but it was beautiful in a different way. Jack stared out the window like a schoolboy, watching every twinkling light, ever horse and carriage, and every child bundled in their winter coats. All of them living their lives to the fullest entirely at the moment. Jack relished in it all.

"Would you like to continue, sir, or shall I head for home?" Larson asked as they pulled up to an intersection.

"Let's head for home. I don't want to keep you away from your family tonight. It's a beautiful night, Larson. You should be with them." Jack answered, turning his attention back to the interior of his car and his driver.

"Thank you, Sir. Home it is. It certainly does feel like there's something magical in the air tonight, doesn't it?" Larson asked.

"Yes, Larson. It truly does."

It wasn't long before Larson pulled the car in front of

the large apartment building where Jack spent most of his time. He owned a large estate home in the suburbs, but with working and spending so many hours with Tabitha, it made sense to stay in town as much as possible. Jack was renting a penthouse loft currently. It had been fully furnished and dreadfully impersonal when he moved in. Not much had changed since. Jack tipped his hat at the doorman as he made his way through the lobby and into the elevator. It wasn't very late, but it was late enough that he was one of the only people milling about. He rode in solitude until finally, he arrived at his front door.

As he entered the apartment, he shed his coat, hat, and left his briefcase on the sideboard table. The sound of his keys hitting the table echoed throughout the quiet apartment. It was a somewhat eerie experience to listen to such an echo from a place that was supposed to provide warmth and solitude. The apartment needed Tabitha's decorating expertise. Without her, it seemed more like a prison than a home.

Jack sighed as he kicked off his shoes and flopped onto the couch, where he grabbed the book on Shinto practices which commanded his attention for the past several months. He read until his eyes grew heavy; then he eventually fell to sleep.

The next morning Jack woke with a start as his book fell from his hands and landed with a surprising thud as it slid across the tile floor. He sat up and rubbed the sleep from his eyes as he looked at his watch. It read 5:30 am. Jack had just enough time to shower and get ready for the day. He stretched and stood to retrieve the book. He didn't often read for fun, but the Shinto customs fascinated him. Even if it was nothing more than superstition from days gone by, the intricacy and delicate nature of which the rituals intrigued him.

He placed the book back in its proper place on the side table and quietly padded across the living room into the master bathroom to ready himself for the day. He chose a smart grey suit and a festive burnt orange tie before jumping into a quick shower. He didn't linger under the lukewarm water; he merely took enough time to rinse the grime of the city off of his skin and out of his salt and pepper grey hair.

He quickly dressed and began to tie his tie when the phone started to ring, interrupting him.

"Odd." He mumbled to himself as he removed the half-finished tie and quickly rushed to the phone in its cradle.

"Hello, this is Mr. Johnson." He answered, a sudden pang of anxiety shooting through his stomach.

"Hello, Mr. Johnson. It's Doctor Foster from Mercy West." The professional monotone voice crackled across the other side of the line.

Jack held his breath. "Yes?"

"Tabitha received some test results this morning, and I'd like to discuss them with you. They are a bit shocking. I called as soon as they came across my desk. I hope I didn't wake you." Dr. Foster explained.

"No, no. I was getting ready to head to the office for the day. Is everything okay? Is she..." Jack began before his voice cracked, and he had to stop.

"Are you sitting down, Mr. Johnson?" Dr. Foster asked.

"Yes," Jack answered, preparing himself for the worst as he grabbed a dining chair to steady himself and take a seat.

"Mr. Johnson, we ran the tests twice to be certain we avoided any errors. We can find no evidence of cancer anywhere in your wife's body. Last week the tumors were there and showed no signs of remission. This week, not a trace to be found. I don't know what beliefs you subscribe to, Mr. Johnson, but I'd call this a gift from God himself. There is no other scientific explanation." Dr. Foster explained.

Jack was speechless.

"Dr. Foster... my wife... is my wife cured?" He

stammered as tears began to flow down his face.

"As far as our medical expertise is concerned, yes. Mr. Johnson, your wife, is cancer-free." Dr. Foster repeated. "We'd like to monitor her for observation just to be certain there wasn't a mistake somewhere, but otherwise, she will be ready to return home after some physical rehabilitation."

"Thank you, doctor. Thank you. I don't know what else to say." Jack wept into the phone.

"I wouldn't thank me, Mr. Johnson. You need to be thanking someone upstairs. I'll be sure to call you and update you with any changes. Have a good day, Mr. Johnson." Dr. Foster said before gently hanging up the phone.

Jack dropped the phone as soon as the line went dead and fell to his knees.

"Thank you! Thank you!" He yelled as he threw his arms up.

He wasn't sure who he was thinking, but it was clear, some divinity had intervened on Tabitha's behalf, and he was overwhelmed with gratitude.

When the tears stopped, he pulled himself up off the floor and retrieved the phone handset that lay where he dropped it. He was still shaking with overwhelming emotions but managed to dial the office number. The phone rang several times until Becky answered with her normal cheerful voice.

"Becky, it's Mr. Johnson. I won't be coming in today. Tabitha..." He started before his voice cracked with emotion once again. He could hardly believe what he was about to say, and the words refused to come out.

"Tabitha? Oh, Mr. Johnson..." Becky answered, fearing the worst.

"No. No, Tabitha is coming home!" Jack yelped with excitement.

Over the next several weeks, Tabitha continued to

flourish. The doctors were entirely baffled. Not only did her physical body begin to heal, but it also seemed that her heart began to improve as well. She was more engaged with the staff and less withdrawn. It took her several months of physical rehab before she was ready to return home, but to see even the little bit of improvement daily was encouraging. Jack still visited her each evening and was instrumental in her recovery.

Finally, the day arrived when Tabitha was ready to leave the hospital, which had been her home for nearly seven years. She was nervous, excited, and apprehensive. She had lost most of her trademark red curly hair during her various radiation and chemo treatments. It had begun to grow back in during her rehabilitation. However, it was now a dull, lifeless bronze. She was thankful to have her hair, but it left her feeling slightly insecure.

She stood in her bathroom, staring at her reflection in the mirror. It had been so long, she barely recognized herself. She could see now why Jack had been so concerned about her as time wore on. She looked like a shadow of her former self, and could scarcely believe that she had survived both her cancer and the traumatic grief of losing their son.

For quite a while, she didn't want to survive. She spent many days willing cancer to spread and kill her softly in her sleep, but then she would always worry about what would happen to Jack if she left him behind. It sounded cliche, but she felt that he completed her soul. They celebrated their tenth wedding anniversary, and she never for a second doubted her decision to spend the rest of her life with him. It was his dedication and love that kept her from completely slipping away over the years.

Her attention left her meager reflection. It focused on the beautiful necklace that Jack delivered to her on the eve before her remission discovery. She only took it off to shower and sleep; otherwise, it was securely around her neck at all times. Even with daily wear, the pendant still shone with an interior luster that she couldn't adequately describe. It was like a piece of the moon had fallen and taken with it the reflection of the sun.

While Tabitha didn't entirely believe in Omamori, Kami, or the Shinto religious beliefs, she did have to wonder.

Her thoughts were interrupted by a gentle knock at the bathroom door.

"Are you ready, my love?" Jack called on the other side of the locked door.

"Yes, I'm almost ready, Jack." She answered, pausing to fluff her short hair and fix her knee-length skirt before opening the door.

Jack was just as dapper as ever in his suit and tie. He'd made arrangements to leave the office early and accompany Tabitha home for which she was grateful. It would be wonderful to catch up with Larson, but she would enjoy Jack's company once she arrived at the house.

Jack reached out and took Tabitha's arm in his own, and together they walked out of her room and through the maze of hospital corridors.

"I'm glad you know where you're going, Jack. This hospital is quite a mess." Tabitha said as she followed her husband around each turn, staircase, and access tunnel.

"I never had to worry about anyone coming to steal you away from me, that's for certain," Jack responded with a smile. "I can't tell you how thrilled I am to have you by my side this time. I'd almost given up hope that you would ever leave this place."

"I'm glad you didn't give up on me, Jack," Tabitha said as the lobby, and the main door of the hospital slowly came in to view.

Suddenly, Tabitha let go of Jack's arm and stood stone still.

"What's wrong, Tabitha?" Jack asked, stopping in his tracks and turning to see his wife's expression. She was as white as a sheet almost as if she had seen a ghost. "Do you need to sit down? Are you okay?"

"I…" Tabitha began, not entirely sure what she wanted to say.

It had been so long since she ventured into the world except for the small view from her window. She suddenly felt afraid and couldn't entirely explain why.

Jack waited patiently for his wife to respond to his questions, and when she didn't, still paralyzed by something unseen to him, he turned and took each of her small hands into his own.

"It's okay, Tabitha. You don't have to go out there alone. I'm here with you, just like I promised I would be." Jack spoke as he rested his forehead against Tabitha's.

Tabitha closed her eyes and smiled as she tilted her head back and gave her husband a gentle kiss.

"You know me so well. I didn't even have to tell you I was afraid." She whispered, squeezing Jack's hands a little bit tighter.

They stood suspended in one another's arms until gently Jack pulled away and led his wife through the main doors and out into the brisk fall air. The bright sunlight hit her eyes and briefly stung. She shielded her face with her arm until her pupils adjusted.

"Are you okay, my love?" Jack asked, still firmly holding Tabitha's hand within his own.

"Yes. I'm okay. Let me have a moment to take it all in." Tabitha answered honestly, giving Jack's hand a gentle squeeze.

She was overwhelmed by the long-forgotten scents of the outdoors. She took a deep breath allowing all of them to flow across her palet and sink into her consciousness. She could smell the smog and pollution of the city, the sun warming the fabric of her coat, her husband's comforting cologne, and a hint of crisp leaves hanging on the nearby trees.

"Okay, I'm ready." She whispered with a broad smile.

Jack returned her smile and led her toward the edge of the sidewalk, where Larson was patiently waiting. Jack opened the door for his wife and helped her slide into the back seat before climbing in himself.

"Mrs. Johnson, it's good to see you. How are you feeling?" Larson asked, turning around in his seat to properly greet Tabitha with a warm, genuine smile.

"Larson, it's wonderful to see you too. I'm well, thank you. How are Jenny, Billie, and Whitney?" Tabitha answered.

"Growing like weeds, ma'am. Can you believe Whitney is a senior this year? She's on her way to graduation with honors. We're proud of her. Billie just started fifth grade. He's doing well in school now. Jenny is having a few minor health problems, but nothing we won't be able to handle. All those years of working at the hotel are starting to catch up with her, I think." Larson answered, returning his attention to the road ahead of him as he pulled into traffic.

"Oh, I'm sorry to hear that. You know, if it's something Jenny might be interested in, I could use some company at the house and help to prepare meals until I get back on my feet. She's always welcome to the position." Tabitha offered.

"Thank you, Ma'am. I'll mention it to her. Are we heading to the apartment or the house, Sir?" Larson asked.

"Let's go home, Larson. I've had my fill of that drab apartment." Jack answered, placing his arm around Tabitha, who had leaned into his chest.

"I've missed this so much, Jack." She said with a contented sigh.

"Me too, my love. Me too." Jack answered.

Soon fall gave way to winter, and with it came the busy holiday shopping season. The Johnson's had settled back into their home, and Jack ended the lease at his downtown apartment. Tabitha spent most of her time in the suburbs still a bit fragile from her extended hospital stay. One afternoon she was feeling adventurous and decided to journey into town to pick up a few things for the large holiday dinner she was preparing.

It was the first time she had visited the city on her own since her illness. She was apprehensive as Larson pulled up to the front of a major chain store situated in the center of the large shopping district.

"Are you sure you're going to be okay, Ms. Johnson?" Larson asked.

"Yes… I can't stay sequestered forever. Thank you, Larson. I'll call you when I'm ready." Tabitha answered, steeling herself and tightening her wool coat around her waist.

"Be careful, please, Ms. Johnson. I'm only a phone call away if you need anything." Larson assured her.

"I know, Larson. You take such good care of me. I appreciate you more than you know." Tabitha said with a warm smile. "Okay, here we go. Off to the holiday shopping madness!"

Tabitha quickly threw open the car door and thrust herself out into the bustling sidewalk. She closed the door and waved as Larson pulled into traffic. Out of nervous habit, she reached for the pendant, which was still securely around her neck. The silver was beginning to lose it's bright luster because Tabitha held it so much, but the chain was strong, and the pendant was robust. It felt comforting between her fingers each time she needed a little bit of courage or reassurance.

Having replenished her courage, she walked confidently into the store and began to collect the things she needed. The store bustled with crowds, and most people had lost any sense of holiday cheer consumed with their thoughts and feelings. Tabitha was jostled and shuffled and bumped into repeatedly before she was finally ready to pay for her things and continue home.

"Thank you. Have a wonderful holiday," Tabitha said kindly to the cashier as she gathered the giant bag of her items and began to head toward the door.

"Sure, whatever." The cashier replied, already moving on to the next guest.

Tabitha scowled as she struggled to hoist the large shopping bag over her shoulder. Once she was successful in steadying the bag, she waddled outside and called Larson.

"Hello, Larson. I'm ready to get out of this mess, and head over to the park for lunch. I'll be waiting outside of the store." Tabitha explained with a grunt as she set her bag down on the sidewalk beside her.

"I'll be there, right away ma'am," Larson answered, before disconnecting the call.

She quietly put her phone away in her small purse and looked up and down the street, hoping to see Larson and the car, a beacon of hope in the sea of pedestrians and traffic. Once again, she reached for her pendant and began to take slow measured breathes. While she had never been an anxious person before, something about her illness and loss changed her. She struggled with racing thoughts and panic attacks often, but she wasn't going to deter from living her life. Having her pendant and practicing some breathing exercises Mr. Johnson had recommended, helped immensely.

She glanced up and down the street once more, and finally caught sight of Larson maneuvering his way carefully through traffic. She hoisted her shopping bag onto her shoulder and stepped to the curb, where Larson expertly pulled directly in front of her.

"Thank goodness, Larson. You have no idea how relieved I am to see you." Tabitha exclaimed as Larson stepped out of the car and opened the trunk to retrieve Tabitha's belongings.

Tabitha handed the large bag to him and opened the door slipping into the quiet sanctuary of the back seat.

"I can imagine Ma'am. It's busy everywhere." Larson empathized, climbing back into the driver's seat and slowly making his way back into the flow of traffic. "You said you wanted to visit the park for lunch?"

"Yes, please. I haven't had a street taco in ages, and I have quite a craving for one." Tabitha answered with a coy smile.

Larson laughed.

"Say no more, Ms. Johnson. I know just where we can find you some street tacos." He replied, shifting lanes and heading toward the park.

Tabitha admired the scenery as Larson navigated the busy city streets with ease. Soon they were pulling into the park. They circled several times until a parking spot opened up, and they both got out and began to walk.

"You don't mind the walk, do you, Ms. Johnson?" Larson asked as Tabitha walked quickly to keep up with his pace.

"Not at all. It's nice to stretch in the open air for once. The store was so crowded and stuffy. I did a lot of walking, but I still felt suffocated. Being out here like this is nice." Tabitha answered, stuffing her hands into the large front pockets on her wool coat. "And please. You've been our driver for nearly a decade. Call me Tabby, or Tabitha if you want to remain semi-formal. We're walking through the park to eat street tacos, Larson. You're my friend."

Larson smiled.

"Alright, Ms... I mean, Tabitha. It's going to take some getting used to." He answered.

"I should have told you ages ago. I was just preoccupied with other things. I apologize. You've been such a blessing to our family. You have." Tabitha explained earnestly.

"Thank you, Tabitha. That means a lot." Larson replied as they reached a small food stand under a large oak tree next to a cluster of small picnic tables.

They waited in line and ordered their food. Once the

meal was ready, Larson and Tabitha made their way to a table by a large oak tree and took a seat. Tabitha unwrapped her food and took a large bite.

"These are delicious. Mmm, exactly what I wanted." She said, finishing her bite and taking a large sip of cola. "It feels good to be out in the city again. I didn't realize how much I missed being locked away in that hospital bed."

Suddenly Tabitha's phone began to ring from inside her purse.

"Oh, excuse me." She mumbled with her mouth full of food as she dug through her purse and produced her cell phone.

She scowled as she read the number across the caller ID. It was her doctor. She considered allowing the call to go to voicemail, but instead slid the icon to the answer position and held the phone to her ear.

"Hello?" She asked cautiously.

"Yes, Mrs. Johnson?" The voice on the other end of the line asked calmly.

"This is Mrs. Johnson," Tabitha repeated, taking a deep breath as her heart began to race.

"This is Ginger from Dr. Albert's office. We received the results from your ultrasound, and I wanted to let you know that you are, in fact, pregnant. It defies every explanation, and odds considering your medical history, but it's confirmed. Congratulations, Mrs. Johnson." Ginger relayed with an excited squeak in her voice. "It appears that you're nearing the end of the first trimester with two healthy embryos."

"Oh.. Oh, my God. Really?" Tabitha exclaimed as tears began to fill her eyes.

"Yes, Mrs. Johnson. Twins!" Ginger repeated.

"Thank you. Thank you! Do I need to make a follow-up appointment? I… I don't even know what to say." Tabitha yelped through ecstatic sobs.

"You call your husband and other family members. I'll

contact you with follow up details later. Have a wonderful afternoon Mrs. Johnson." Ginger replied before she ended the call.

Tabitha held her phone, sobbing, and shaking, unsure of what to do or what to say as she noticed Larson's look of concern.

"Is everything okay, Tabitha?" He asked as he set down his food prepared to give her his full attention.

"Yes. Yes! Larson, everything is wonderful! I'm pregnant with twins!" Tabitha yelled as she leaped from the table and grabbed Larson's hand. Tabitha ran into the small meadow beyond the oak tree Larson following closely behind. Once they reached the open sky, Tabitha threw her arms skyward and spun around in a giddy dance.

"Thank you! Thank you!" She yelled at the top of her lungs. "This is the best day of my life! I am so happy!" She screamed as tears continued to flow down her face.

Soon the burst of energy born from her excitement waned, and she became light-headed.

"Oh. I need to sit down." She laughed as she plopped unceremoniously into the grass. "Larson, please call Jack. I want him to meet me here so I can give him the news. I want him to hear it here in this gorgeous sunshine."

"Right away, Ms. Johnson. Er... Tabitha." Larson answered as he pulled his phone from his pocket and dialed the number to Mr. Johnson's office.

Tabitha threw herself back into the grass as she took several deep breaths, trying to compose herself. As she did, the clasp on her necklace which had previously held so strong, broke. The weight of the charm pulled the delicate chain from around her neck, and when she finally sat up to follow Larson back to the car, the necklace fell to the ground.

3 SHOPPED AND DROPPED

The necklace lay in the grass as time passed. It reflected the sun and moon as they rose and fell each day until it disappeared in a cover of fresh snowfall. Time continued to march forward until the snow eventually gave way to mud and rain. Still, the necklace and charm dutifully reflected the light and glistened with the same inner glow with it had been forged.

After an unusually cold blustery day, a starling swooped down from its perch in the old oak tree to investigate the flickering light coming from the grass. It tilted its head, pecked cautiously, hopped back and forth, and eventually decided to grasp the delicate chain within its beak. It struggled to become airborne with the length and weight of the chain, but after a few fumbled attempts, it finally took to the sky.

It flew away from the park, through a maze of highrise buildings and continued even beyond the suburbs until it reached a small rural town and its nest in a comfortable maple tree. Its partner was anxious to get away from the chicks and happily surrendered the nest once the starling toting the necklace arrived. Before it began to warm the new hatchlings, the starling carefully wove the chain into the outer branches of the nest. It left the pendant hanging just low enough to catch the light from the setting sun.

A crisp spring breeze swayed the pendant back and forth as the starling settled in to keep her hatchlings warm.

Billy pulled his rusty old pick up truck off of the small country road and into his worn gravel driveway. He paused just inside the driveway, hopped down, and peered into the mailbox. Billy found nothing of interest as he flipped through several bills, and other junk mail before jumping back into the truck and continuing down the dusty old drive. He just finished a double shift at the factory. He was more than ready to be home, kick off his work boots, and relax with a cold beer.

As he pulled around the house back to the garage, something caught his eye in the old maple tree. It looked like a light, or reflection of something shiny hanging from one of the lower branches where the starlings usually kept their nest.

"I wonder what those damn birds have dragged into my tree this time," Billy mumbled to himself as he parked the truck and silenced the old diesel engine.

He hopped out of the cab and made his way to the tree where he could see a small shiny object dangling precariously from a starling nest. He hoisted himself up into the tree using the full low fork. He cautiously made his way as close to the nest as possible without disturbing the starling and her hatchlings.

"What have you got there, Mama Starling? I don't think you need any fancy jewelry." Billy said as he reached up and grasped the hanging pendant. With great care, he slowly unwound the chain from the branches and finally freed the necklace in its entirety.

"Huh, where did you find this Mama Starling? It looks custom made." Billy mused mostly to himself as the starling squawked and protested Billy's invasion of her nest while he examined the necklace more closely.

It was dirty and weathered, but not beyond repair. Billy tucked it into his coat pocket and climbed down from the tree before heading inside the house. The rusted old hinges on the door protested as he pushed his way into the kitchen. The old farmhouse had been in his family for three generations, and he hoped to pass it down to his daughter Kelsey eventually.

"Billy, is that you?" Ann, Billy's wife, called from the laundry room.

"Nope. It's your other husband." Billy answered with a chuckle.

"Thank God. I didn't want to see Billy's ugly mug tonight anyway." Ann teased walking into the kitchen with an overflowing basket of laundry precariously balanced on her hip. "There is a plate left for you in the oven. Kelsey didn't come home again last night."

Billy pulled a dining chair away from the dining room table. He collapsed onto it the weight of work and the news that his daughter hadn't come home, falling squarely on his shoulders like a boat dropping anchor.

"Was she out with Justin again?" He asked, bending over and removing his work boots.

"I'm not sure. Probably. Kelsey didn't show up to work last night, either. Pam called here looking for her. Are we worried about this yet, Billy?" Ann asked, setting the laundry on the table and collapsing in the chair closest to Billy.

"I don't know anymore. Kelsey's eighteen, we can't legally tell her what to do or not to do. I don't think we can file a missing person report until she's gone for something like forty-eight hours. How long has it been?" Billy answered, standing from his chair and setting his boots next to the door before wandering to the oven and grabbing his leftover plate and casually tossing it into the microwave.

"It will be forty-eight hours at 7 pm," Ann answered, beginning to fidget with a decorative napkin holder sitting on the table.

"Okay. We'll go from there." Billy answered, glancing at his watch. The hands were just about to turn to 6 pm.

"Okay," Ann answered as she stood from the table and snatched the basket of laundry to take upstairs.

Billy stared out the window, willing his daughter to pull in the driveway safely until the microwave beeped and broke his concentration. Having been brought back to the present, he removed the plate from the microwave and sat back down to eat his dinner.

Ann was an excellent cook. Even reheated, the beef roast, mashed potatoes, and cornbread warmed Billy inside and out. Taking each bite, he understood why southern style cooking equated to comfort food. Billy couldn't think of a better way to soothe his worry than with Ann's roast and cornbread. As he finished his meal, he again glanced at his watch. The minute hand was ticking precariously close to 7 pm, and still, no one had heard from Kelsey.

To be sure his watch was accurate, Billy pulled out his phone as well. The display confirmed his fears. It read: 6:58 pm. He pressed the home button and clicked on the phone icon, poised to dial the local police dispatch. He hesitated a moment before entering the number he had memorized from Kelsey's wayward youth. Just as he was about to hit the send key, he heard a crash from behind the house.

"Billy?" Ann called from upstairs.

"It wasn't me. I'll check it out." Billy called back, grabbing the revolver he kept stowed on top of the refrigerator and slowly heading out the backdoor to investigate.

He held the gun pointed down next to his side. He slowly walked to the corner of the house, quickly surveying the rest of the property and listening for any indication of what might have made the noise. He checked the side mirror of his truck, hoping to get a glimpse behind the house before he had to expose himself to any potential threats. When he didn't see anything obvious in the reflection, he raised his weapon. He sprang from behind the house to find Kelsey collapsed in a heap next to several spilled trash cans.

"Kelsey Lynn! What on earth?" Billy yelled as he immediately dropped his revolver and slid it into his pocket.

When she didn't respond, he ran to her side and quickly rolled her over. Her clothes were covered in vomit and reeked of stale cigarette smoke and alcohol.

"Kelsey? Are you okay? Kelsey! Can you hear me?" He called, checking for signs of life.

She was breathing, and her pulse was erratic but steady.

"Daddy?" She croaked as her eyes fluttered open, and she struggled to sit up.

"Good Lord, child. What have you gotten yourself into?" Billy sighed, half angry at the condition his daughter arrived in and half relieved to see her alive at all.

"I just went to a party with Justin. I guess I got a little drunk." Kelsey slurred.

"Billy? Is everything alright?" Ann called from the kitchen doorway.

"Yes! Everything is fine. It was Kelsey." Billy called back before turning his attention to Kelsey and softening his voice. "Come on. Let's get you cleaned up. You've been missing for almost two days. What the hell were you thinking?"

"Two days? Fuck, I was supposed to work last night." Kelsey mumbled as Billy helped her to her feet.

"Yeah, you won't have to worry about work for a while," Billy answered. "That was your last warning."

"Uuuuuugh! What the hell? It was just one shift. I've been on time every other day in like forever!" Kelsey yelled, stumbling over her feet.

Billy quickly put his arm around her to steady her as they

both walked into the house where Ann was impatiently waiting.

"Kelsey Lynn! Where have you been? I've been worried sick about you!" Ann yelled as Kelsey stumbled up the small stoop and into the kitchen.

"God, mom. I was at a party with Justin. I'm fine."

"You're covered in vomit and smell like an ashtray. Did you walk home like that?" Ann asked, rushing to steady her daughter.

"I don't know. Leave me alone, Mom. I'm going upstairs." Kelsey mumbled, pulling away from her mother before stumbling up the stairs and slamming her bedroom door.

"Well... we found her." Billy said with a heavy sigh.

"Billy, she wasn't drunk. Was she high?" Ann asked, wringing her hands with concern.

"I think so, but on what I don't know. Kelsey is lucid. That's all that's important. We can check on her before bed." Billy said as he pulled his wife into a protective embrace.

They stood silently, unsure of how to help their child until the old grandfather clock in the living room began to chime. The loud, steady rhythm brought them back from their worried thoughts to the present situation.

"You better get ready for bed. I'll get your lunch together. Your clean laundry is sitting at the foot of our bed." Ann mumbled, as she wiggled out of Billy's arms and continued to busy herself with menial household tasks.

"We'll figure something out, Ann. She's home safe for now. Let's focus on that tonight." Billy said softly before turning on his heels and slowly lumbering up the staircase.

As he made his way across the landing, he wandered by Kelsey's room. The door was standing slightly open, and he peered inside. He found her passed out again, this time across her floor. She had soiled herself, but he could see her chest rising and falling with steady breathing. He closed her door completely, shook his head, and continued to the master bedroom at the end of the hall, where he sat on the edge of his bed.

He didn't understand where he failed as a father to have his daughter wind up in a puddle of excrement on the bedroom floor. He thought he did everything right. He checked up on her grades, he got to know her friends and kept track of what she was into online and elsewhere. She seemed like such a happy, good kid until two years ago when she started spending time with Justin. Suddenly, his happy go lucky little girl became withdrawn and sad. She started missing school and work, and her friends, sense of style, and interests changed dramatically. Billy recognized that something was wrong. Still, he had no idea how to help, or even address the issue when he couldn't be sure he even knew what the problem was in the first place.

The more he thought about it; the heavier his heart became until he could hold his emotions back no longer. He buried his face in his hands and wept.

The next morning the bedside alarm echoed off the walls with a shrill siren. Billy was not prepared to wake up and begin his day. He flung his arm in the general direction of the bedside table, hoping to connect with the alarm clock and silence the piercing noise. After several attempts, he was finally successful, and a peaceful silence settled over the room. Ann was sleeping peacefully beside him. He never understood how she could sleep through his various alarms over the years, but wake up the moment Kelsey tossed in her bed.

Billy rolled to his back and stared at the ceiling as his eyes adjusted to the dim moonlight filtering in through the small bedroom window. The sun hadn't even begun to cross the horizon, but duty called. He slowly tossed off the comforter and swung his legs around to the edge of the bed. Before his feet hit the cold hardwood floors, he stretched his back and neck, which issued several sharp cracks in protest. He scratched what little remained of his receding hairline, and willed himself to stand up and head to the bathroom to begin his morning routine.

As he was walking across the room, he shuffled through his dirty laundry and stepped on something cold and sharp.

"Ouch!" He hissed in a whisper as he stumbled in the darkness.

He continued into the bathroom. He turned on the light, opening the door wide enough that the illumination spilled outward into the pile of laundry. As he did, he caught a glint of something reflective. He paused, allowing his eyes to adjust to the light before taking a few steps and reaching down to retrieve the necklace he'd found in the starling nest the day before.

"Oh. I'd forgotten about you." He whispered to the necklace that seemed to glow even when it wasn't reflecting any direct light source. "Huh."

He took the necklace into the bathroom with him and gently laid it on the vanity while he continued his morning rituals. He quickly showered, shaved, and dressed for the day ahead. Before he left the bathroom and headed downstairs, he scooped up the necklace and slid it into his pocket. Kelsey's birthday was coming up, and he wanted to have the jewelry cleaned and repaired for her. He wasn't entirely sure what else to do with it anyway. Ann wasn't a fan of silver, and he didn't think it was worth enough to sell or appraise. Even if it had been at one time, it certainly wasn't now after being liberated from the starling nest.

Billy lumbered down the stairs and headed to the kitchen, where he put on a pot of coffee and quickly prepared a peanut butter sandwich for his lunch. As he stood by the counter, Kelsey slowly stumbled into the kitchen. At some point during the night, she had finally recovered from her stupor and cleaned herself up. Her hair still wrapped in a bath towel with a few damp ringlets poking their way out. She was in clean pajama pants and a tank top.

"Hi, Daddy." She mumbled. "Can I have some coffee?"

"Hi, Baby Girl. Sure, let me grab you a mug. What happened at that party with Justin the other night? You came home quite a mess." Billy answered as he took a clean mug from the dish strainer and filled it half full, leaving room for sugar and cream.

"Uuuuuugh… I don't even want to talk about it. It was great for a while, but then I… well, you saw me." Kelsey answered honestly.

"Yep," Billy answered, unsure of how to propel the conversation any further.

What could he say to her that wouldn't make her angry, or run off right back into Justin's arms? They sat in awkward silence as both of them sipped their coffee until the time came for Billy to head to work.

"Well… I'm heading out to work. What are you doing for your birthday next week?" Billy asked as he pulled his coat from the hook and slipped his arms into it.

"Oh, I don't know. Probably nothing. Maybe go out." Kelsey answered, still nursing her coffee and staring blankly at nothing in front of her.

"Maybe your mom can bake you a red velvet cake. Is that still your favorite?"

"Yeah. Sure. I guess. You're going to be late, dad." Kelsey answered as she pulled her cell phone out of her pocket and began to hit the keys.

Billy nodded as he glanced up at the clock hanging above the stove, then headed out the door and across the driveway to his truck. The sun was beginning to peek over the horizon, and the frost scattered across the lawn and freshly plowed fields next door glistened with a red-orange glow. Soon everything would be blossoming, then turning a lush shade of deep green. Billy longed for the summertime. It was his favorite season, and with it came memories of young Kelsey playing carefree in the yard, catching fireflies, or chasing dandelion seeds.

He signed and climbed into his truck. The low rumble of the tired diesel rattled the windows of the house. Billy could hear the neighbor's dog barking as he pulled out of the driveway and made his way down the narrow country road into town.

Once he arrived in town, he stopped at the local gas station, picked up a newspaper, and a cup of stale black coffee. After making his purchase, he returned to his truck and made his way to the factory where he had spent the majority of his adult life. The security gate clattered and squeaked in protest as it slowly opened before Billy passed through. He was the first one there, as usual, so he had his choice of parking. He circled the lot once and settled on a space before turning off the engine and opening the newspaper to peer at the classified ad section.

He was looking for a jeweler who might know how to identify the necklace he'd found, or at least help him get it clean and packaged for Kelsey's birthday. The only jeweler he'd known had long since retired, and he hadn't required anyone since. He flipped through two pages of ads before one stood out to him. He hastily wrote down the address and phone number as he finished his coffee; then made his way inside the factory to begin his workday.

The workday went by quickly. Billy recently celebrated his twentieth anniversary at the factory. The work he did was monotonous, putting a bolt on a nut day in and day out, but the pay and benefits were worth it. Plus, the job may have been uninteresting, but something was comforting about settling into a predictable routine. He enjoyed being able to do his job well while also having a lot of time to contemplate. Once he was at his work station and placed his OSHA required ear protection on, it was like he was in his little bubble until the last bell rang for the day, and he had to return to reality.

The bell rang, and he carefully shut down his machine before stowing his ear protection and heading out the door. Once he arrived at his truck, he hopped in, checked the time on the dashboard, and headed back through town to the address listed in the paper. Jefferson's Jewelry Palace was just off the main highway in the same shopping plaza as the only local big box store in the area.

As Billy drove, he wondered why he hadn't seen the store before. Something with a name like Jewelry Palace should have stood out.

"Huh… I don't know how I missed that." Billy mumbled to himself, focusing on the road in front of him.

Traffic through town was hectic in the late afternoon. Most factories and warehouses in the business park had shifts that ended at the same time. The population of the city might have been on the small side, but you'd never know it if you arrived in town at the right time during the day. He sat impatiently through several traffic lights until finally, he was able to pull into the large parking lot at the shopping plaza. He found a reasonably close parking spot, stowed his truck, and made his way into Jefferson's.

"Hello, can I help you?" A kind young woman asked as soon as Billy stepped through the door.

"Yes, please. I found this necklace on my property. It was picked up by a Starling. I was wondering if you might be able to help me figure out where it came from and get it cleaned up." Billy explained, pulling the necklace out of his pocket and showing it to the young woman.

She took the necklace and held it up to the light. It sparkled and issued an iridescent glow beneath the layers of tarnish.

"Hmm…. it doesn't look like it's mass-produced, but I can't see any distinguishing hallmarks on it either. Can I clean it up and get back to you?" She asked, pulling glasses on her head down to the bridge of her nose and squinting at the necklace.

"How much will that cost me?" Billy asked as a matter of fact.

"Oh, nothing upfront. If we find a hallmark and can get a hold of the original owner, there is no need to pay for something that is going to get sent away." She explained, bringing the necklace down and carefully laying it across the service counter.

"How much will it cost if you can't find the owner?" Billy asked again.

"With this level of tarnish? Probably $65 for cleaning and anywhere up to $100 for cleaning and repairs." She answered.

Billy thought about it for a moment. He had no idea what a reasonable price for such services might be, but he wanted to give the impression that he did.

"Okay. That sounds reasonable. Is it silver?" Billy asked.

"Yes, sir. Under all of that tarnish, it appears to be silver." The salesperson answered.

"Perfect. When can I expect to have it back?" Billy asked.

"Let me take a look here..." The salesperson said as she pulled out an appointment book and flipped it open to the correct date. "It looks like we can have it back to you by Saturday, or at least have some answers for you by then. Will that work?"

"Yes, that's great," Billy answered, smiling.

Kelsey's birthday was on Sunday. If everything worked out, the necklace would be the perfect present for her.

"Wonderful! Just let me take down your information, and we'll get started on it right away." The salesperson said, grabbing a pen and opening a screen on her sales computer. "If you'll just write down your name, address, and a good phone number for me, we'll be in touch."

Billy obliged, finished leaving his information, and headed out to his truck.

The salesperson watched as Billy walked to his truck and pulled out of the parking lot before carefully scooping up the necklace and taking it to the backroom where Steve, the silversmith, was working.

"Here, Steve. This necklace just came in. Can you clean it up and see if there might be a hallmark on it? Some farmer brought it in and said he found it in a bird's nest or something. Will you run it through the database and make sure no one is looking for it?" The salesperson instructed as she placed the necklace onto his workbench.

"Hmm…" Steve said as he set the piece he was working on aside, and picked up the necklace. "This is some fine craftsmanship. Someone is missing this little beauty."

"That's what I thought too, but the guy seemed genuine. Let me know, okay? I told him we could have it ready by Saturday."

"Saturday? Jill, I have ten other pieces I'm working on right now. I can't just stop everything for this." Steve protested.

"Look at it, Steve. This necklace is a priority. It practically glows on its own. This one is special." Jill retorted.

Steve let out an angry sigh and went back to his work, waiting for Jill to lose her patience and storm off like she usually did. The two oldest employees of Jefferson's were always at odds with one another. Jill had no respect for Steve and his craft, and Steve had to patience to deal with the public and their often unreasonable demands. If they weren't bickering about one order or another, it wasn't a typical day at the office. Jill eventually rolled her eyes and returned to the front of the store to tend to her other duties.

"Heh… typical." Steve huffed as soon as Jill was out of earshot.

He paused in the progress he had made on the piece he

was working on, to examine the necklace more carefully. As soon as he picked it up, a cold chill ran down his spine, and a soft breeze flowed through the workshop.

"Well, now, you are a special one, aren't you?" Steve spoke eyes wide with surprise.

Intrigued by the reaction he had to the necklace, he put the previous piece away, and began to change out his tools. Jill was right. The necklace took top priority.

He carefully cleared away the dust and debris left from his previous work and took out a new vice and polishing wheel. Something was on the pendant, but it was covered with dirt and tarnish. The inscription was impossible to read.

He placed the pendant into the vice. He dipped a small corner of the polishing cloth into a cleaning solution before carefully applying the cleaning solution to the necklace. He let it sit momentarily to breakdown the oxidation, then wiped the dirt and grime away, leaving the beautiful sheen of clean sterling silver behind. He applied cleaning solution again twice more until the Kanji finally shone through in all of its majestic glory.

"I'll be..." Steve gasped once the inscription became clear. "I haven't seen this script since 1975, and is that... is that niello? You're a little piece of magic; it is what you are. Jill! Come here!" he yelled.

Jill made her way to the backroom and Steve's workbench.

"What did you find?" She asked.

"This is an Omamori charm. It means happiness, and it was carefully handcrafted. I didn't find a hallmark anywhere on it, unfortunately, but if you believe in magic, this piece found its way to the person who needed it most." Steve explained.

Jill scoffed at the idea of magic, or an inanimate object having any say in destiny or fate.

"Well, that's ridiculous, but if you didn't find any

identifying hallmarks, I suppose I'll have to return it to the gentleman who brought it in. Will you have it finished by Saturday?" She huffed.

"Yes. I'm going to finish it today. You might not believe in magic, but I do. This little charm has a story to tell. I only wish I could understand it." Steve mused as he continued to clean the charm delicately.

Jill didn't reply. Instead, she returned to the front service counter and her sales duties leaving Steve to himself as he turned the charm over and continued to remove the tarnish carefully. Once he finished with the pendant, he slid it off the chain and turned his attention to examining each link for damage that needed repair.

For being discovered in a bird's nest, the chain was in remarkable shape. Whoever owned the necklace before it found its way to the starlings had taken great care of it. Once he inspected the chain for any damage, he set about cleaning it. The chain was a much more tedious task than the pendant as it had many small spaces for oxidation to creep and bind between the links. After pulling a cleaning swab out of his tool kit and running over the links by hand, Steve pulled out the ultrasonic cleaning machine he employed for difficult cleaning tasks such as these.

He measured out the necessary amount of solution and added the chain before closing the lid and setting the timer. The small machine whirred to life, and Steve returned to the pendant. He was unable to use the ultrasonic cleaning machine due to the application of the niello. However, he wanted to make sure that every speck of dust or dirt came clean before the charm would return to its new owner.

He bent over and shuffled through a crowded and disorganized drawer in his desk until he found the tool he needed. It was a water pick, often recommended in dental offices, to use in place of floss. He filled the reservoir with distilled water, placed several shop towels down across the workspace, and pulled out his third-hand stand to which he carefully installed the pendant. Once he made sure the pendant was secure, he pulled his LED headlamp with attached magnification glasses over his head and went to work.

With the increased magnification, he could see each intricate stroke left behind from several different size gravers. Whoever crafted the pendant was a master craftsman. Steve wished that he or she had left a hallmark. Regardless of where the necklace wound up after he was finished cleaning and restoring it, Steve would love to meet and learn from someone who created such a unique piece and with such great care.

Steve began to smile as he watched the small particles of dust and debris melt away under the gentle stream of water. The charm was exquisite, and he was honestly surprised by how well the sterling had held up after such severe oxidation. It only served to solidify his assessment. What he was working on was nothing short of a little piece of magic.

Just as he finished with the pendant, the ultrasonic cleaning machine beeped, signaling the completed cycle. He quickly cleaned up his workbench and removed the chain from the device. It sparkled as if it was diamond, an incredible sheen that he had never seen before from sterling. He lay it across a towel and dried it with great care. When he was satisfied that the chain was dry, he married it to the pendant once again. As soon as the decoration slid to the middle of the chain, he closed the clasp.

A cool breeze swirled around him, sending yet another chill down his spine. He shivered slightly and pulled out a blue velvet box bearing the emblem of Jefferson's. As he placed the necklace into the box, he noticed that it seemed to possess an internal glow. It wasn't just reflecting the light; it was a source of light.

He shook his head in disbelief; then closed the box.

Billy was already well into his workday when he noticed

his phone vibrating in his pocket. He usually didn't have the opportunity to stop production at his station and check his phone. Still, with Kelsey's recent lapse in judgment and odd behavior, Billy made an exception. He shut down his machinery for a moment and pulled the phone from his pocket to view the caller ID. He was surprised to see the number for Jefferson's flashing across the screen. Noting that it wasn't urgent, Billy returned his phone to his pocket and restarted the machine. The jewelry store could wait until after his shift was over.

At the end of the day, as he was heading out, Billy pulled his phone out and dialed the number to his voicemail. He was expecting to hear that they had discovered a hallmark on the necklace and planned on returning it to the rightful owner. To his surprise, the salesperson, Jill, he had spoken to just yesterday, was informing him that the necklace was ready for pick up. They hadn't found distinguishing marks, and all he had to do was arrive at the shop.

He wasn't expecting the project to be done so quickly, especially since they had estimated it would be ready Saturday. Receiving the phone call on Wednesday afternoon was a pleasant surprise. He thought about calling and letting them know that he would stop by after stopping at the bank, but in the end, he decided to go about his business. The necklace wouldn't go anywhere, and he didn't like talking on the phone anyway. He was a face to face business person. To him, phones, computers, and other forms of impersonal communication were pointless and crude. The only proper way to close a business deal was with a handshake. You couldn't deliver a handshake over the phone.

Billy hopped into his truck and didn't waste any time pulling out of the parking lot and heading toward town. First, he stopped at the bank and withdrew the proper amount to cover the cleaning bill. While Jill hadn't indicated the total cost of the services, Billy remembered that she mentioned it wouldn't be over $100. He took out $150 to cover any additional fees or taxes and headed over to the shopping plaza.

Once he arrived, he parked the car next to the curb and made his way inside the small shop.

"Hello?" He called upon walking into the building. He thought it was kind of odd that no one was there to greet him this time around when Jill had been so prompt the other day.

"Hello, Billy! I'm so glad you received my message. Look at what we have here for you. It looks like an entirely different piece now that it's been cleaned up." Jill answered, popping to the front of the store through the small swinging door leading to the back stock and work area.

She held a small blue velvet box that she set on the counter and motioned for Billy to open.

Billy took her cues and opened the box.

"Wow." He gasped, seeing the necklace's bright sterling reflect the fluorescent lights with a unique sheen.

"It's it beautiful? Steve, our resident silversmith, said it's the Japanese character for happiness, and it's supposed to bring the wearer many blessings. It was handmade, and great care was taken to craft it. Unfortunately, the hallmark has either worn off or never engraved into the pendant." Jill explained.

"Yes, thank you. It is beautiful. How much do I owe you?" Billy answered, still entranced by the necklace.

"As we discussed since we didn't need to make any significant repairs, the base price for cleaning is $65. Let's get you rang out. Can I help you with anything else? Maybe a nice pair of earrings to compliment the necklace?" Jill offered, taking the necklace back from Billy. She walked down the service counter until she reached the register and typed in several codes until a price populated on the display where Billy could read it.

"No, thank you. The necklace will be fine. My daughter's

birthday is on Sunday. I want to give this to her, but I'm not even sure if she'll wear it. I don't know her very well anymore." Billy lamented as he pulled out his wallet and handed over a crisp $100 bill.

"I'm sorry to hear that…" Jill said with a very fake look of concern across her face as she took the bill from Billy and made the correct change out of her cash drawer.

Billy issued an equally forced, polite smile as he accepted the change across the counter.

"Thank you. It looks wonderful. Have a good one." Billy said with a slight nod of his head as he scooped the blue box off the counter and tucked it safely into his coat pocket.

Jill said something as Billy walked out the door, but he wasn't listening. They did a fantastic job cleaning the necklace, but he was less than impressed with Jill's customer service skills. Billy wouldn't be returning to Jefferson's anytime soon. He would be happy to get home after a long day at the factory.

He climbed into the cab of his truck, placed the necklace securely in the glove box, and started his journey home.

It didn't take long until Billy was rumbling down the driveway toward the house and barn. He was so glad to see his little homestead appear on the horizon each day. It wasn't much, but it was his, and Billy worked hard for it. Coming home each night was a privilege that he didn't take lightly. Billy pulled into his usual parking spot and silenced the engine. He gathered his lunch box and leaned over to retrieve the necklace; then he thought better of it. Billy would leave it inside the truck so he could surprise Kelsey with it on her birthday. If he took it inside, he was likely to give away the secret or have Ann discover it before it was time to give it to Kelsey. He smiled as he patted the glove box and climbed out of the truck before making his way into the house.

Not ten minutes after Billy closed the back door behind him, Kelsey stumbled out of the barn. She was beginning to experience the worst part of withdrawing after Justin had convinced her to take a hit of methamphetamine at the party several days before. Now she was searching for anything that she could pawn or sell for scrap at the local junkyard to satisfy her craving.

When she didn't find anything in the barn, she was about to give up. Then her dad pulled in the driveway and stashed something in the glove box of the truck. She couldn't see what he was doing, but she figured she would give it a try. Maybe he had a paycheck or something else of value in the truck. She felt a small twinge of guilt as she climbed up into the cab, but her guilt was overwhelmed by the sickness of withdraw beginning to take over her system.

"Holy shit." Kelsey gasped as she opened the glove box and found the small velvet jewelry box. "Jackpot."

Kelsey snatched the jewelry box. She stuffed it into her coat pocket, before slamming the glovebox and jumping down from the cab and climbing into her small sedan. Kelsey took a deep breath to steady the dizziness consuming her head and wiped the sweat off of her forehead. She started the ignition and sped off heading toward the only pawn shop in town.

"Where is she off to in such a hurry? I didn't even know she was home?" Billy asked as he watched Kelsey fly down the driveway through the small kitchen window.

"I don't know. Maybe she went to work? I think she was in the barn looking for something before you pulled in." Ann answered as she sat a plate of hot food down on the table both for herself and for Billy.

"Huh," Billy mumbled before sitting down to a quiet dinner with his wife.

Kelsey struggled to stay centered on the road. The longer it took her to get to the pawnshop, the sicker she was becoming. She had heard about withdrawing from Justin's friends, but she had never thought that just one hit could have such a detrimental effect. Her skin felt like a million ants were crawling underneath it. All she wanted was to scratch at them, but she had to keep both hands on the steering wheel or risk running off the road. The more she tried to focus on the lines in front of her, the more they seemed to blur.

"Come on, Kelsey. Keep it together." She mumbled to herself as she took a deep breath and slowed to a stop at a four-way intersection. She glanced in her mirror first than to each side of the intersection. When she didn't see any other traffic, she took a moment to pause at the stop sign. She closed her eyes and took a deep breath while absentmindedly scratching at a single spot on her arm until it began to bleed. Soon her focus was interrupted. Another car pulled up behind her and issued a quick blast from its horn.

She jumped, waved an apologetic wave, and continued through the intersection. She was only a few miles from town now. It was still early in the evening. She would have plenty of time to pawn whatever was in the jewelry box and head across town to pick up Justin from work to get her fix. The last five miles of her journey seemed to stretch into infinity. She could see the speedometer registered 45 miles per hour, but it felt like she was crawling down the road at a snail's pace. Time, in general, felt distorted and wrong. Even as she watched the dial on the dashboard clock click from one minute to the next, her perception skewed.

Finally, she reached the small Back Alley Pawnshop. It was a stereotypical pawn shop. A small stone building with iron bars covering each of the small windows and plate glass door in a less than desirable part of town. She parked her car haphazardly in front of the building and crawled out the driver's door. Her legs were weak, and the dizziness was almost unbearable, but she managed to steady herself and walk into the shop, jewelry box in hand.

"Can I help you?" A gruff gentleman asked as soon as Kelsey stumbled into the door.

"Yes!" Kelsey yelped. "I mean... yes. I want to sell this. Or pawn it or whatever. I need cash. I have this." She rambled as she pulled the jewelry box out of her pocket and handed it over to the skeptical man from behind the counter.

He looked her up and down as she continued to fidget nervously. He knew she was coming down off some illicit substance, but the jewelry box intrigued him. He flipped it open and carefully removed the necklace from it's home.

"This looks like a pretty special necklace. Are you sure you want to part with it?" He inquired, admiring the quality of the craftsmanship and luminosity of the necklace.

"Yeah. I never wear the thing. It's just been sitting in that box. I need money." Kelsey mumbled as she began to grow more and more uncomfortable, the longer the gentleman behind the counter continued to watch her.

"Alright. Let's get you written up. You have any ID on you?" He asked, returning the necklace to the box and pulling out a small receipt pad.

"Oh... crap. I left my purse at home. Is that going to be a problem? Please, I need this money. I don't have enough gas to get back home. I live out in the country. I need gas." Kelsey lied.

"You don't need gas, honey. You need drugs, and I'm not in the business of supplying junkies with their next fix. When you have your ID, I'll be happy to buy this from you, until then you're out of luck." The man scolded as he tossed the jewelry box across the small counter in Kelsey's general direction.

She caught the box as it tumbled across the counter, and collapsed to the floor where she began to sob erratically.

"I need gas to get home, mister. Please. I need gas to get home!" Kelsey wailed, committed to her lie, and desperate as her discomfort increased with every passing moment.

"No. Get the fuck out of here." The man huffed as he walked into the backroom and returned with a cordless telephone receiver. "You've got five minutes to get up and get out, or I'm calling the police and having you arrested for trespassing."

Kelsey looked directly into his eyes as her tears continued to fall. She struggled to stand but eventually accomplished the task and walked out of the small shop. She hopped into her car and recklessly sped away, never noticing that she dropped the tiny box onto the floor and left it behind.

4 RE-GIFTED

"What the hell? That dumbass junkie dropped her necklace." George, the owner, and proprietor of Back Alley Pawnshop, grumbled as he wandered out from behind the counter to retrieve the small blue box.

"What was that, hun?" Nancy, George's wife, called from the back room. "Who did what now?"

"Eh, some junkie came in here without an ID trying to sell this to me. I told her to leave, or I'd call the cops, so she bolted, but she left the damn thing behind anyway. It's her loss. It's a beautiful piece. Probably stolen, but beautiful." George answered, handing the box to Nancy and returning to his seat behind the service counter, where he had a football game playing on a small black and white television.

"Wow. Should I call Bill and see if it comes up in any database as missing?" Nancy asked, admiring the necklace before closing the box and setting it back on the counter.

"Nah, there's no hallmark on it. The box is from Jefferson's, but I've never seen anything of this quality come through here out of Jefferson's. She probably just found the box or had it lying around. She doesn't deserve to have this if all she's going to do is sell it for drug money.

It's Omamori. It needs respect." George explained as he turned his attention back to the football game.

"So technically stealing it from a junkie is more respectful than trying to return it to her?" Nancy smirked.

"You can't steal a genuine Omamori. It goes where it's needed. She dropped it. It belongs here. If I remember right, the Kanji means happiness. We sure could use a little happiness in this joint." George argued, ignoring Nancy's smirk and taking the box off the counter and tucking it behind the cash register.

"Okay, hun. Whatever you say." Nancy finally relented as she returned to the backroom and auditing their inventory.

Back Alley Pawnshop had been an institution in the small town for as long as Nancy could remember. George worked there from high school on and eventually took over after the original owner passed away two years previously. Ever since, they had been pinching pennies to get by. With the opioid epidemic sweeping across the country, no one was interested in buying any of the used wares that came into the store; they were only interested in selling them. Some months they barely broke even, let alone made any healthy profits. Nancy knew this shop was essential to her husband, but she wasn't sure how much longer they could survive this way.

George was well aware of the state of his finances. Still, at 45 years old with no high school diploma, he didn't see many other options for gainful employment, especially in the tiny town consumed by drugs and petty crime. He was going to hold out as long as he could with Back Alley Pawnshop.

Nancy loved her husband, and she was content to stay by his side no matter what happened to their little shop. She was growing worried as she continued recording the inventory. She counted several old guitars and noted them in her ledger before moving to the smaller items. Each item was tagged and matched to a receipt, the expiration date, and any payments or remainder left on balance.

She pulled a small catering cart behind her. Each time she came across an item that was due to move to the sales floor, she made a note and piled it onto the cart. So far, she had only encountered five items that were current on payments, and her carriage was nearly full. She glanced up from the ledger and looked at all the shelves she had yet to inventory. They were out of space. If they didn't begin moving items off the sales floor soon, they would be unable to buy anything, leaving them in financial ruin.

Nancy shook her head and continued with her inventory duties. Soon she was finished going through the stock room and sat down at her computer to log everything into the new electronic tracking system she was implementing. As long as Nancy could remember, George had carefully cataloged everything by hand. But when she began helping at the store, she decided to put her programming degree to good use. It didn't take her very long to put a simple tracking program together. The most challenging part of the project had been entering inventory and making sure the numbers on the receipt tags matched the numbers handwritten on the item tags.

Once the program opened, she carefully set her ledger next to the keyboard where she could read the numbers and type unobstructed with the ten key keypad. Since she had taken over the inventory, she made sure to organize most items in numerical order. It wouldn't take long for her to type in the correct codes. She could use the ten-key pad with her eyes closed if she had to as long as her data was sequential. She took a deep breath and set about working through the ten pages of her ledger just as George wandered into the back room.

He looked at his wife with her fingers flying across the keys as she quickly flipped through each page of her ledger. She only paused once or twice to double-check herself when a small red box popped up on the computer screen. He smiled as she continued her work.

George admired his wife so much. She had started at the bottom of her chosen profession immediately after high school and worked her way through college. She could do anything if she put her mind to it, and George was lucky to have her. Their life together hadn't been without its struggles. Soon into their young marriage, they discovered that they could never have children of their own. They considered adoption, but with George's only experience being in pawn and Nancy's wages barely enough to cover the bills on her own, they had been unable to.

It motivated Nancy to continue her education, but it sent George deeper into depression. He felt useless and as if he was holding Nancy back, but he couldn't bring himself to make any significant changes to his life. Now, they were married the better half of 30 years, and Nancy had retired from her career with a good retirement income and spent her time helping George with the shop. It was too late to make any meaningful change.

George huffed, frustrated with himself once again, and walked past his wife to collect his coat and other belongings. The business day was over, and he was heading home.

"Watch yourself when you leave, Nancy. That junkie might come back looking for her necklace. I'll see you at home." George grumbled as he walked out the back door.

He made sure it locked securely, and that all of the security bars were in place before he climbed into his old sedan and pulled away from the shop.

"If that junkie comes back looking for her necklace, she'll be out of luck," Nancy mumbled to herself. She pulled the small blue box out from its hiding place behind her computer monitor. "You're going to auction tonight, little necklace. Something has to pay the bills around here."

As soon as she was sure George left for the evening, she

closed her electronic tracking program and pulled up a popular online auction site. She pulled the cart full of inventory closer and put together several lots of various items, taking a few pictures with her cell phone before listing them on the site.

She could never tell George that she was auctioning off stock to pay the overhead and keep the store open. It wasn't that he would disapprove, it's that he was strictly old school. She knew he felt powerless and often worthless the farther into debt the store began to sink. It was the best solution that she could come up with that wouldn't damage her husband's already fragile ego at this difficult transition in his life.

Much to her surprise, before she could even finish listing all of the inventory she planned to liquidate, a notification tone rang through the quiet shop. She pulled out her phone and to her surprise, saw that the lot of miscellaneous jewelry items she just finished listing sold almost immediately.

"Well, now, that's a nice surprise. We can keep the lights on this month." Nancy said to herself as she gathered each item listed in the lot and put them aside into a small box. She would ship them on her way home.

She remained at the shop watching various listings to see if anything else would sell, and when the clock struck 9 pm, she decided it was time to pack up and head home. She tucked the box of jewelry under her arm and quietly left the shop, making sure to remain vigilant as she walked down the alley to her car.

Much to her relief, she had the alley entirely to herself and made it safely to her car without incident. Not wasting any time sitting in the lane, she quickly pulled out on to the deserted main street. It wasn't very late, but on this side of town everything and everyone generally packed up before dark. If you didn't, you were risking robbery, muggings, or worse.

Keeping her location in mind, Nancy slowly rolled through most intersections and red lights until she passed the train yard. Once Nancy made her way into a more affluent part of town were families were milling about on the sidewalks visiting restaurants, cafes, and small businesses. It was almost like driving into a completely different world. Nancy often considered looking into a space for the shop over on this side of town, but pawn shops came with a certain stigma attached to them. She doubted that the city council would approve of their move. It was still something to keep in the back of her mind if the auctions ever stopped bringing in enough income to pay the bills.

She pulled into the small post office parking lot, parked, and made her way inside with the small package securely under her arm. She paused at the small packaging counter. She grabbed some parchment paper and several bubble mailers to ensure the contents of her package arrived in the same condition she was sending them in. After carefully wrapping each item and replacing them into the box, she taped it up, paid for the necessary postage, and slid the box into the package drop.

"Good luck, little package." She whispered as she peered through the package drop to make sure the box had fallen safely into the postage basket.

The package sat in the collection bin until early the next morning when the first postal employees arrived at the post office. It was weighed, postage double-checked; then it was loaded onto a semi-trailer where it spent several days jostling around as it traveled hundreds of miles. Eventually, the truck came to a stop at another small post office, and the package was unloaded and tossed onto a conveyer belt for sorting.

It was weighed once again, scanned, and sent to the

correct shoot lined up with many other packages and letters scheduled for delivery. It sat on the shoot for several hours as each other package and letter was carefully sorted and bundled before being loaded into a postal truck. Soon it was lifted from the shoot and tossed haphazardly into the back of a postal truck. The door was closed, and off it went bumbling along in the trailer until it reached its final destination: Brighton Coin and Jewelry.

"Here you go, ladies." The postal carrier chirped, placing the package and several other small mail items on the sales counter before waving and dashing back out to his truck.

"Thanks, Sam," Charli called with a wave as she collected the packages off the counter and took them to the back stock room. "We have gifts!"

Charli distributed one piece of mail to each of her coworkers, keeping the large package from Back Alley Pawnshop for herself. They each opened their perspective packages and compared contents.

"Here's the utility bill. Any bets to how much we spent this month?" Brenda laughed as she waved the bill over her head before placing it on her desk in the correct filing box.

"I have that shipment of solder for Herb." Cathy laughed, setting the box on a shelf.

"And I have this wonderful lot of antiques. Look at these, girls." Charli squealed with excitement. "I bid on them last week. This lot is perfect just in time for the holidays. There are some nice pieces in here."

Each of the Brighton team crowded around Charli as she unpackaged each item.

"These earrings are darling, aren't they?" Charli said, holding up a delicate pair of gold earrings with small rubies set in the center of the post. "And this bracelet is stunning."

Charli was in charge of purchasing. She loved the thrill of finding a good bargain, and unique pieces to stock her vintage counter each season. Brighton was a small midwestern city, and Charli had spent a good majority of her adult life there. She was well connected in most of the city social circles, and always knew how to keep a steady flow of customers with her inventory choices. It was almost second nature. While she never pictured herself in the vintage and antique market before she retired from her medical coding career, she did thoroughly enjoy it.

"Ah, here it is." Charli beamed with a smile as she pulled out a small blue velvet box and opened it to find the necklace. "This one is for me, girls. I honestly can't believe I was able to find it stateside. Look how beautiful the craftsmanship is."

Charli passed the box around to each of her coworkers that all admired the necklace with equal astonishment.

"Charli, that is gorgeous! Is it for you or Nate's girlfriend?" Brenda asked, intrigued.

"I don't know yet. I originally bought it for Jen, Nate's girlfriend, but this is so much more intricate than I ever imagined. I might keep it for myself." Charli answered honestly with a small chuckle.

After the staff continued to inspect the rest of the packages and log them into inventory, they returned to their various duties across the store. Charli made her way to the vintage jewelry counter, where she carefully arranged her new stock. The day passed slowly, but soon it was time to pack up and head home for the evening. Charli rang up the necklace and clocked out. She made sure to stow the small box in her purse before making her way out into the busy pedestrian city center. Her car was parked just a few blocks away, but in the hustle and bustle of the holiday shopping season, it seemed to take ages before she arrived.

The wind was brisk, and the air held the scent of impending snow. Charli felt refreshed and excited about the upcoming holidays. Nate, her son, had been away from home for several months, pursuing his latest career interest by enlisting in the National Guard.

Nate was closer to 30 than 20 and had been struggling

to find his place in the world after high school. She was proud of him for at least continuing to try different career paths, but she was sad that her little boy was still struggling to fit in. Not only was the National Guard his sixth attempt at a lasting career, but he had also been ostracized by his peers most of his life. He struggled with learning disabilities and social delays making the sweetest, genuine little boy grow into a tired and often depressed young man.

His inability to find a lasting career cost him his first marriage. He was in a holding pattern of self-destruction, a revolving door of young women, and financial struggles. Jen had been by his side through most of his efforts after losing Sarah, which Charli could respect and appreciate. However, she knew that Nate wasn't genuinely committed to Jen. The brief conversations that Charli overheard between Nate and his father regarding Jen deeply troubled her. She sat on the sidelines during most of Nate and Jen's tumultuous relationship. However, the more she got to know Jen, the more troubled she became at the way her son was treating her.

That's why she purchased the necklace she found browsing around on auction sites for her latest holiday inventory. Her husband had briefly been stationed in Japan during his military service days. He brought back many cultural customs and trinkets with him. One of the most poignant for Charli had been the Shinto custom of the Omamori. Charli had never seen such intricately crafted Kanji stateside until she stumbled across this necklace. The rest of the jewelry in the lot was unimpressive, and she would be lucky to sell it off during the holiday shopping season. Still, for this necklace, it was worth taking a loss.

A small shiver ran down her spine as she climbed into her sporty coupe and closed the door quickly after her. She only lived about three blocks away but chose to drive due to the unpredictable weather. Unfortunately, since she didn't have far to drive, her car would not have time to properly warm-up before she arrived.

"It's days like these I miss Florida," Charli mumbled to herself, rubbing her hands together as the car engine roared to life.

She soon pulled out into traffic and made her way home. She parked in the garage and was pleasantly surprised to see that her husband was already back from work. Wes had retired from his military career several years previously. Still, he kept as busy as humanly possible, and she rarely saw him during the week. She admired him for remaining dedicated to self-improvement after his retirement. Yet, she wished that he would slow down just a little bit and spend more time at home. In a way, she felt like she barely knew the man whom she had been married to for the better part of forty years. If you accounted for all of his time spent abroad or deployed for various assignments, they probably only spent about half of that time together in any capacity. He always thought of her while he was away, and always returned with something special. He made time for her and Nate when he could, but sometimes Charli still felt left behind.

She parked quietly in the garage and made her way inside the house.

"Wes?" She called as she set her purse down on the kitchen counter and continued to the living room looking for her husband. "Wes, are you home?"

"Hmm. I'm in the office, Charli." Wes answered.

Charli followed his voice and found her husband with his head buried in a book and various computer programs open across his monitor.

"What are you doing, dear? I didn't expect to see you home this early." Charli asked, putting her arm around Wes' shoulder.

"Oh, I just had to finish this project, and I left my manual at home," Wes answered, distracted, barely acknowledging his wife.

"I see. Dinner will be ready in about an hour. Come up to eat when you're done. I picked up Jen's gift at work today. I want you to look at it." Charli said, removing her arm from Wes' shoulder and wandering back into the kitchen where she opened the fridge and stared at its contents, willing a recipe to jump out at her.

Eventually, she chose the ingredients for a green salad, baked chicken, and baked potatoes. It wasn't the most lavish meal, but it was quick and relatively easy to prepare. She pulled the necessary pans and utensils out of various drawers and set about with the preparations.

In no time at all, she had shredded the lettuce and added cucumbers, tomatoes, carrots, and radish to the salad bowl. The potatoes were sliced and snuggly wrapped in foil marinating in garlic butter, waiting for their turn in the oven as the chicken finished roasting on the broiler.

"It smells wonderful, dear," Wes said as he made his way through the kitchen and sat down at the small dining table with his face still buried in a programming manual.

"Thank you. It's not much, but you won't starve." Charli answered as the alarm on the stove sounded indicating the chicken finished, and the potatoes were ready to go in. "Everything should be finished in about twenty minutes. Do you want a glass of wine while we wait?"

"No, thank you. Wine with dinner will be fine. Have you heard from Nate today?" Wes asked, finally setting his manual aside and removing his glasses before rubbing his eyes.

"No, why? Should I have?" Charli asked immediately concerned for the well being of her son.

"He said he might call to set up the arrangements for transportation from the airport today. I just wasn't sure if he had or not." Wes answered.

"Oh. No. I haven't heard. I thought Jen was picking him up?" Charli asked as she poured herself a glass of white wine before joining her husband at the dinner table.

"I'm not sure. Nate said he wanted to surprise her since he was coming home a few days early. I don't think he'd want her to pick him up if that was the case." Wes explained.

"God only knows what he has up his sleeve at this point." Charli sighed.

"True," Wes answered. "I wish he would settle down. He's not getting any younger, and neither am I. I don't know how much more of his antics I can tolerate."

"They aren't antics. Nathan is trying. You know how much he struggles with school. At least he isn't dealing with drugs anymore." Charli snapped back, chastising Wes for his harsh judgment of their son.

"Yes…" Wes began, trying to figure out what to say that wouldn't hurt his wife, but remain valid. "At least there's that. He's not a child anymore, Charli. I won't be around to bail him out forever. After the hoops we had to jump through to get him into the Army, if this doesn't work out there's nothing left I can do to help him. He's already burnt through over half of his inheritance in the last two years alone, and I'm not even dead yet."

Charli knew her husband was right, but she still hated to hear him speak about their only son in such a flippant and dismissive manner, especially when Nate was going through an especially challenging time in his life.

"Have some faith in our son, Wes. Maybe he wouldn't be struggling so much if you weren't so hard on him." Charli quipped as she finished her glass of wine and returned to the kitchen to check on the potatoes.

"I'm sorry, dear. We won't discuss it any more tonight." Wes finished, retrieving his manual from the sideboard where he had stored it and returning to his work.

Charli huffed from the kitchen and poured herself another glass of wine. She drank quickly before pouring another and realizing she had almost drunk the entire bottle by herself.

"Great." She muttered under her breath. "That's all Nathan needs. A father who's given up on him and an alcoholic for a mother."

She put her wine down on the counter and continued preparing the meal. Her anxiety was already triggered, and she was shaking.

A few days later, Nate finally called his mother. He made arrangements for Wes to pick him up from the airport and return him to his car so he could surprise Jen at her apartment if Jen were willing to see him. Nate wasn't sure, but he heard rumors that Jen had been seeing another man while he was gone. He was only half hoping to surprise her for legitimate reasons, and was half expecting to catch her in the act so he would have an excuse to end the relationship.

While he was away, Nate had met someone else. Originally it wasn't his intention to see other people while they were apart. As soon as he saw Molly, it was like the rug was pulled out from under him and he fell head over heels. He knew he needed to end the relationship with Jen, but he didn't know how to stop it. He'd always been honest with her about his feelings, and for some reason, it just wouldn't sink in with Jen. She loved him, but he didn't share her opinions. Of course, he liked her. She was fun to be with, cute, and the right partner for some of his more hairbrained business adventures. But he could never get past the fact that he didn't have that head over heels instant connection with her.

He could be happy with Jen; that much was sure, but he would never share the electric connection he had with Molly. That was what he craved more than anything else in a lifetime partner. Further complicating matters was the fact that Molly was married to someone else. They were separated and headed for divorce when Nate first entered her life, but there was no guarantee that she wouldn't change her mind and go back to her husband.

Nate wasn't prepared to throw away what he had with Jen until he could be confident that what he had with Molly would last. So he was stuck, looking for any excuses to drive Jen to leave him, or at least initiate a break to ease his guilt for pursuing a relationship with Molly.

All of this was running through his head as he sped down the interstate late one night after his flight landed, and he picked up his car. He told Jen that he would be coming back to town on the 19th, but had arrived one day earlier. It was past midnight when he finally made his way to her apartment, but it was still a day before she was expecting him.

Instead of calling her to see if she was awake or would even be home, Nate just decided to show up. He dragged his suitcase up the flight of stairs leading to Jen's apartment and quietly knocked on the door. When she didn't immediately answer, Nate decided to knock again this time a little bit louder. Still, he received no answer and began to rock nervously back and forth from one foot to the other. Finally, Nate knocked one last time and prepared to grab his bag and head back to his parents' house. It wasn't, mainly what he wanted to do. Still, if Jen refused to answer the door, he wasn't obligated to continue the relationship. Maybe it was a blessing in disguise. Maybe Jen had been seeing another man, and he was there right now.

Before Nate could finish his thought, the door flew open and Jen threw her arms around him while rubbing the sleep from her eyes

"Nate! You're home early!" She yelled, still struggling to wake herself from sleep.

"Yeah. I'm a little early. I didn't think you were going to let me in." Nate answered, returning Jen's hug and offering a small kiss.

"I'm sorry. I wasn't expecting you. I didn't know who was knocking on my door. I'm so glad you're home." Jen answered as she took two steps back and allowed Nate to drag his suitcase inside, shutting the door behind him.

"I'm happy to see you," Nate said quietly.

"Come to bed. I have to be at work in a few hours." Jen mumbled, still fighting sleep from her eyes.

"Yeah... I think I'll sleep on the couch." Nate answered quietly.

"What? Why?" Jen asked, confused more than offended.

"I don't know. I just got used to sleeping on those hard military beds. I think the couch will be more comfortable." Nate lied.

"But I've missed you," Jen said, standing on her tiptoes to reach up and give Nate a passionate kiss.

Nate returned her kiss, then pulled away with a nervous chuckle. "I've missed you too, but I think we need to talk about some stuff. I want to wait until tomorrow for that."

"Okay, whatever. Well, I'm going to bed. You can join me if you want or sleep on the couch." Jen said with a scowl. She waved her hand and made her way back to bed.

Something was bothering Nate, but Jen was too tired to sit down and drag it out of him. He would come around and tell her when he was ready.

She climbed under the covers and closed her eyes until she was roused awake by Nate shuffling into the room. He shed his clothes and climbed into bed, where he immediately rolled Jen onto her back and began to kiss her neck.

"I thought you said you wanted to wait until tomorrow and talk about things?" Jen asked as she arched her back and leaned into Nate's kiss.

"Eh... I changed my mind. I missed you." Nate answered as he slowly undressed Jen.

"I missed you too," Jen answered as they fell into the quiet rhythm of intimacy.

The next morning Jen woke early and headed off to

work. She hated leaving the quiet security of Nate's warm embrace. Unfortunately, her vacation wasn't scheduled to begin until the day after, and it couldn't change. Her shift flew by, and finally, it was time to go back and spend the rest of the week with Nate and their families celebrating the holidays.

Jen bounced up the stairs and into the apartment, thrilled to see her boyfriend sitting quietly on the couch watching TV. It was a sight she had sorely missed while he had been away.

"Hey, babe." She called from the entryway as she shed her coat and shoes before heading down the hall to change out of her work uniform and into something more comfortable.

"Hey, how was work?" Nate answered, not taking his attention away from the TV.

"Pretty good," Jen answered as she made her way back to the living room now dressed in a comfortable sweater and yoga pants as she let her hair down and curled up on the couch next to Nate. "So, you said you wanted to talk to me about something last night. What's up?"

"Oh… yeah, nevermind. It's nothing." Nate answered as he put his arm around her.

"Oooookaaaaay…" Jen answered as a twinge of anxiety flowed through her stomach.

"Don't worry about it, Jenny. It's okay. It's the holidays. Let's enjoy them together, okay?" Nate reassured her, noticing the concerned look flash across her face.

"Yeah… Okay. So what are we doing for dinner? Are you hungry?" Jen asked, content to change the subject.

"I don't know. What to go out and get something?" Nate answered, pulling Jen a little bit closer.

"Sure. Fast food?"

"Sounds good to me. Anything is better than military food." Nate answered with a smile.

Jen retrieved her shoes, and Nate followed closely

behind as they headed for the door and down to Nate's car.

Dinner was uneventful. Jen could sense that something was troubling Nate, but anytime she tried to bring it up, he would change the subject or ignore her entirely. She was thrilled to have him home and busy planning their time together, but still, the lingering tinge of anxiety wouldn't leave her alone. After they finished their meal, they headed back to Jen's apartment, where they climbed into bed and lay next to one another, simply basking in their togetherness.

Jen was thrilled and peaceful snuggled underneath Nate's arm. She missed listening to his steady heartbeat as she fell asleep each night. As far as she was concerned, they could lay in bed together for the duration of his stay, but they had plans for the majority of his stay. They were planning on visiting with Charli and Wes the next evening.

"So... Remember what I wanted to talk to you about?" Nate asked, breaking the silence that had fallen over the pair as they drifted toward sleep.

"Oh... no, what's wrong?" Jen answered, her heart skipping a beat.

"Well... okay. So there are a lot of parties on base during the weekends. I don't have to be on base if I don't want to, and one weekend I got drunk and ended up at this house with a bunch of other people. I woke up the next day in bed with this girl. I felt awful. I never wanted to hurt you. I mean.. Honestly, I kept calling her Jen. That was the first thing she asked me when she woke up. 'Who's Jen?' And I answered: 'That would be my girlfriend back home.' So... I just wanted you to know that. I never, ever, ever tried to hurt you. I feel terrible. Like... I feel awful. God, I feel horrible." Nate stammered quickly.

Jen took a deep breath and began to weep softly into Nate's chest. He was holding her tightly to his body out of fear or protection; she wasn't sure.

"I'm so sorry, Jen. Are you okay?" Nate asked after

allowing Jen a few moments to process the terrible news he had just delivered.

Jen lay silently. Her head was pounding, her heart was racing, and her chest was heaving with muffled sobs. She didn't know if she was okay. She had never experienced such a betrayal from someone she loved so dearly. The pain was almost too much to bear, but instead of telling Nate the truth, she sat up, wiped her tears, and said: "It's okay. We never discussed what we would do during our time apart. If you want to sleep with other people while you're gone, I don't mind. Just don't get her pregnant, and don't bring her home. What happens there stays there. When you come back, we can start fresh."

Nate stared at Jen in complete disbelief.

"Are you serious?" He asked as he gently grabbed Jen's face and turned to see her eyes.

"Yeah. I don't mind. Just be safe." Jen repeated, eyes still wet with tears as her sobbing finally came to a complete stop.

"Holy shit. You are serious. God, I love you." Nate reiterated as he pulled Jen close once again and quietly held her until she fell asleep.

Nate couldn't seem to find sleep, even after Jen was softly snoring beside him. They had plans to meet his parents the next day for brunch before heading out to the local mall and picking up a few last-minute gifts. He didn't understand why or how Jen could be okay with the fact that he cheated on her. He could see that she was upset. She was crying as he told her the details of his infidelity, but she still forgave him.

It frightened him. Not only did he not understand it, but he was afraid. Maybe Jen's love wasn't genuine. Perhaps she was using him, and that's how she could overlook his poor treatment and brazen infidelity. He didn't know what to do. Wes had always encouraged him to be honest with Jen about his feelings. Still, whenever he tried, she always reacted as if it was no big deal, or like he was telling her one big joke. Nate felt trapped, and the longer he stayed in bed next to Jen feeling conflicted and uneasy, the more he longed to be back on the base next to Molly instead.

Morning arrived, and they rose together slowly. Nate hopped in the shower, and Jen lingered in the bed, basking in the warmth of the sunlight filtering in through the window. She was okay with Nate doing whatever he wanted to while he was away. Jen knew he had a voracious sexual appetite. While she longed for him to be faithful while he was away, she never honestly expected it of him. She was impressed that he had the guts to tell her about his misdeeds with another woman. He'd never been so straightforward with her, even though she knew he had been unfaithful before during their short time together.

She appreciated his effort to be honest about it, and felt somewhat okay with it all after hearing the truth. She suspected the moment he came home and didn't immediately follow her into the bedroom that he had been with someone else. When he said that he wanted to talk, it only confirmed her suspicions.

She listened to the water gently falling in the tub and the muffled squeaks of Nate's feet as he washed the previous day's grime away before heading off to his parents' house. Jen was excited to see them for the holidays again. She wasn't super close to any of Nate's family, really, but she looked forward to the opportunity to get to know them. She generally enjoyed spending time with them, and it was fun to listen to the stories Charli brought home from her shop.

Nate took after his mother more than his father. Watching Charli's mannerisms and personal flamboyant spunk reminded Jen of an effeminate Nate. They even shared the same squinty smile and razor-sharp sarcasm. Charli could be critical sometimes, but she was fun to be around. Jen had been invited to a lunch and spa date not long before Nate left for his training. She had yet to follow up and make a date. Life and work had kept her occupied since Nate's departure. She barely had time to take care of herself, let alone find time to meet up with Charli.

"Are you ready to go, babe?" Nate called as he turned off the water and stepped out of the shower.

"Just about," Jen called back as she finally rolled out of bed and began to gather an appropriate outfit to wear.

As fun and charismatic as Charli was, and as much as Jen enjoyed spending time with her, she also had very high standards for personal appearance. In a way, Jen respected her for it. It also added a small twinge of anxiety anytime they went out together. Eventually, she chose a nice pair of jeans and a casual red sweater.

"What do you think?" She asked as Nate wandered into the room, wrapped in a towel.

"You look fine," Nate answered bluntly.

"Just fine? Great." Jen snapped back.

"I didn't mean it like that. You look outstanding in jeans. I wish you would wear them more often." Nate clarified. Still, semi distracted as he pulled his jeans out of his suitcase and quickly dressed.

"Not according to your mother." Jen huffed with a frustrated sigh.

"Don't worry about what my mom thinks. You look nice today. I like it. When did you get that sweater? I don't remember it." Nate encouraged, finally giving Jen his full attention.

"Oh, I got it at that new store that opened across the street. It's kind of like that discount retailer, but the clothes are a little bit nicer. We'll have to go over there while you're home," Jen answered as she quickly applied eyeshadow and mascara and slid into her boots. "Alright, this is as good as it's going to get. Let's go."

Nate smiled and gave Jen a reassuring squeeze on the

shoulder before they headed out the door.

The drive to Charli and Wes' home was uneventful and rather quiet. Nate was distracted, and Jen was still emotionally exhausted from his confession the night before. She wasn't angry, and she wasn't despondent, she just felt very, very tired as if her emotional being was dying or giving up. She felt like a giant weight was on her chest, and she couldn't escape no matter which way she turned. Yet, she still held out hope that after Nate returned when he finished his training, things would get better. She could envision better days just on the horizon if only she could pull through this rough patch.

Soon they pulled into the driveway. Nate parked the car, and they both walked in together.

"Nate, Jen. How are you?" Charli called as she finished the last remaining preparations on the dish she was focused on.

"Hey, Mom," Nate called as he continued through the foyer into the kitchen.

"Jen, how are you, dear?" Charli asked as Jen followed Nate into the kitchen.

"Doing well," Jen answered, trying to put on a smile, but falling flat.

Charli looked at Jen and could immediately tell she was stressed and unhappy, as usual. She seemed exceptionally tired this particular afternoon as if something was troubling her.

"Come here, dear. I have something for you." Charli said, walking into the living room and picking up a small gift box before returning to the kitchen.

Jen graciously accepted the gift, and set it down on the counter next to her purse.

"Well, go on. Open it." Charli insisted.

"Oh, well… okay." Jen said, hesitating and glancing across the room to Nate, who only shrugged.

She carefully loosened the small silk ribbon that held the

golden cardboard box in place and opened it. She found a little blue velvet jewelry box nestled quietly inside. She pulled the box out. She opened it to find a beautiful sterling silver necklace with an intricate pendant reflecting brightly back at her.

"Wow. Thank you, Charli." Jen gasped.

"You're welcome. Isn't it beautiful? I saw it come in with a new inventory order, and I just knew you had to have it. It's Japanese and means 'happiness.' You deserve happiness, dear. Don't you think so, Wes? Doesn't she deserve to be happy?" Charli explained as Jen gently took the necklace out of the box and put it around her neck.

"Oh, yes. Of course. Kesley deserves to be happy. She deserves loyalty and honesty, and someone who treats her well don't you think, son?" Wes answered, sternly addressing Nate, who had begun to fidget.

"Dad… really?" Nate fired back at his father, avoiding the question.

Jen could see how uncomfortable Nate was and quickly wrapped her arms around his neck, giving him a small kiss.

"I am happy. Nate makes me happy. He treats me pretty well." Jen said with a smile as Nate avoided eye contact with her.

"Well, no. I don't think…" Wes began before Charli interrupted.

"Wes, help me carry this food into the dining room, would you?" Charli said, handing her husband a large plate of casserole.

"We have champagne to go with brunch tonight. I think you'll like that much better than the Riesling we had last year, Jen. It's bubbly and fun." Charli called artfully, directing the conversation away from the conflict between her husband and her son.

"That sounds wonderful, Charli," Jen replied, trying to lighten the mood and joke with Nate, who had hopped up onto the kitchen counter and wrapped the ribbon from the gift box around his head.

"I am the perfect present," Nate called.

"You are. You're my perfect present." Jen laughed as she pulled her phone from her purse. "Hold still. I want a picture of this."

Nate responded by making a goofy yet strained face as Wes wandered back into the kitchen and leaned against the counter delivering a stern gaze in his son's direction. Nate had spoken to his father about Molly when they met at the airport.

Wes was unimpressed with the fact that his son chose to pursue a relationship with another woman before ending his current relationship with Jen. In reality, Wes had been encouraging Nate to end the relationship with Jen almost as soon as it began. Not because he didn't think very highly of Jen, on the contrary, he adored her. He also knew Nate wasn't committed to the relationship, and that his son had sexually abused her on at least one occasion. Considering his son's past transgressions, the abuse was probably a regular part of the relationship between Nate and Jen.

Wes clenched his jaw as he thought back to the first night he was made aware of Jen's plight.

Nate showed up unannounced at the house very early one morning. Wes was an early riser by most standards, and Nate had arrived even before his alarm went off. As soon as Wes made his way downstairs for his morning coffee, he found his son sitting anxiously at the kitchen table.

"Nathan? Are you okay, son?" Wes asked, immediately on alert. Nate looked like he had seen a ghost. He was pale and looked like he hadn't slept all night.

"I… I messed up, Dad." Nate stammered.

"Do we need to go to the police, Nathan?" Wes asked, trying to imagine what his son could have gotten himself into this time. "Do you need money? What's going on?"

"This girl moved in with me. We fell asleep in my bed. I

rolled over and thought she was Sarah. I think I raped her, Dad." Nate squeaked.

"You, what?!" Wes bellowed in shock. "What do you mean, 'you think'? You either did, or you didn't, Nathan."

"Don't fucking yell at me! I don't know! I'm scared, Dad." Nate fired back as his voice cracked with emotion.

Wes took a deep breath, closed his eyes, and pinched the bridge of his nose as he did his best to regain his composure.

"Okay, Nathan. What the hell happened?" Wes asked, pulling out a chair and sitting down next to his son.

"Like I said. I thought this girl was Sarah, so I started touching her and everything, and she didn't say no or ask me what I was doing so things progressed and then we're fucking, but then all of a sudden she starts crying. So I stopped, and she just curled up in a ball and kept crying. But she didn't say no, Dad. She didn't stop me. I didn't even realize it wasn't Sarah until we were already in the middle of everything, but then I thought okay well what the hell, right? She didn't stop me until she started crying anyway. So I left and came straight here. I don't even know if she's still at the apartment. I don't know if she'll be back. I don't fucking know what the hell I just did, Dad." Nate explained, his voice shaking and a cold sweat spreading across his forehead.

Wes carefully listened to his son, then shook his head, trying to process everything Nate had just confessed. He had no idea what to do or say to his son. It wasn't the first time Nate had admitted a major crime to his father, and Wes had a feeling that it probably wouldn't be the last, but he was still at a complete loss.

"Well… I don't know, son. You have to talk to her. Tell her the truth. If it was truly a case of mistaken identity, then…" Wes trailed off, unsure of how to correctly advise his son in the situation. "You said she moved in with you. Are you dating?"

"No. I met her at work, and her mom was treating her like shit, so she said she wanted to kill herself, and I had the extra room, so I offered to let her move in with me to get away from her mom." Nate explained.

"Okay. So this girl… No, she has a name. What's her name?" Wes asked still struggling to wrap his head around everything his son had just dumped onto his emotional plate so early in the morning.

"Jen." Nate answered.

"Jen moved into your spare room. Why was she in your bed?" Wes asked.

"I don't know. She just never set up the other bed or moved any of her stuff in, so we've just been sharing a bed." Nate replied, beginning to fidget in his seat.

"But you're not dating. You invited Jen into your bed, but you're not dating. What were your intentions, son?" Wes asked as the severity of the situation became clear.

Nate's face became pained as he avoided eye contact with his father.

"I guess I wanted to hook up with her, but I wouldn't do anything like that without asking first. You always taught me to ask. I know that. I… She looks so much like Sarah, Dad. Like so much like Sarah." Nate stammered.

"Nathan, she never should have been in your bed without clear boundaries or a discussion prior. You need to talk to her. Right now. Go home and talk to the girl. If she was crying, she's scared. You hurt her, son." Wes instructed sternly. "Go make it right."

"I have to work in like an hour. I don't have time." Nate argued, looking at the clock.

"Make it right, son," Wes repeated as he rose from the table and walked into the kitchen where he began to make his breakfast.

"Dad?" Nate said, following Wes into the kitchen.

Wes ignored him. The discussion was over, he was mad, ashamed, and embarrassed. If he continued, he would either start yelling, and wake Charli or say something he would regret.

Nate waited a moment for Wes to answer, and when he didn't, he quietly left.

"Can you take a picture for us?" Jen asked Wes, snapping him back to the present.

"What? Oh. Of course." Wes answered, taking the phone Jen had offered him.

Jen made her way back to Nate's side, and they both smiled. Wes clicked the shutter button that appeared on the touch screen, but the phone wouldn't cooperate.

"Did you get it?" Jen asked as her smile began to fade.

"The center button on the screen, right?" Wes asked as he adjusted his glasses in an attempt to see the small icons scattered across the phone screen and making sure he hit the right one.

"Yes. That's the one." Jen answered.

"Okay. Let me see. I think I got it, but I'm not sure. Let me try again." Wes said before the flashbulb lit up the kitchen. "Oh, there it goes. Let me get one more."

Jen and Nate smiled, but their smiles were flat. Both of them had a lot on their minds. Wes could tell, but Jen was pleased with the photo, and that was all that mattered.

"Brunch is ready, let's eat everyone," Charli called from the dining room. She had been busily setting the table and pouring the champagne.

Jen, Nate, and Wes filed into the dining room and took their seats. Wes issued a quick blessing and served the food. Jen cautiously took a small sip of champagne.

"There, that's better now, isn't it?" Charli asked with a smile.

"Yes. Much better." Jen answered with a smile.

"One of these days, we're going to have to go out for mimosas and a spa date, Jen. Just us, girls. It will be fun." Charli said with a smile as she raised her glass in a toast to

Jen.

Jen smiled and returned the toast.

The rest of the meal was relatively uneventful, and soon Jen and Nate made their way home. Jen was glad to retreat to the safety of her home. The afternoon spent with Nate's parents had been pleasant. However, the stress from Nate's previous revelation still weighed heavily on her heart.

As soon as they walked in the door, she made her way straight to the bedroom where she stripped out of the day's grime and wear and quietly climbed into bed. It was fairly early, but she was exhausted. Nate made his way into the living room after shedding his coat and shoes and flipped on the television, where he mindlessly flicked through channels. Unlike Jen, he was wide awake with anxiety and anticipation toward the days ahead. He had one more week of holiday vacation before he would return for his last stint in training.

Everyone he had spoken to about Molly had told him the same thing: He needed to end the relationship with Jen. After the awkward confrontation with Charli and Wes, Nate felt even worse about the situation than he did before. He knew it had to end, but he couldn't bring himself to do it. Nate didn't know what to say, or where to even begin. He assumed confessing his infidelity would end the relationship on its own. He never imagined that Jen would take the news so well and also offer him the option for an open relationship.

"Hey, come to bed," Jen called her eyes heavy with sleep from the hallway.

"I'm not tired," Nate answered. "I'll come in after a while."

"You don't have to sleep. I want you next to me. I don't get you for too much longer." Jen said.

"You have no idea," Nate mumbled under his breath as he stood to turn off the TV and join Jen.

5 MOVING ON

The next week Jen spent with Nate was awkward and strained. He spent less and less time with her and more time alone. Jen could sense the end of the relationship was near. Though Nate had never said it, she could feel it. He hadn't been the same since he returned home for vacation. Coupled with the fact that he had been unfaithful, Jen knew. She wasn't ready to accept it until one night when Nate left her alone and spent the evening with a few of his friends. He said he would be back within an hour, but time wore on, and Nate didn't return.

Jen had called him repeatedly, and he had yet to answer. One time someone picked up the phone, but instead of speaking to her left the line open. She could hear Nate in the background speaking with someone else. That someone else sounded like a woman; then she heard Nate pick up the phone and end the call. She immediately called back, but this time the phone went directly to voicemail.

She was livid, and hurt, and betrayed, and sad, and confused all at once. Not only had Nate lied to her about spending the evening with his best friend from high school, but he was ignoring her calls as well. He was ignoring her to spend time with another woman. Not hundreds of miles away, but right here in Jen's back yard. Suddenly she knew what she had to do. She jumped up and gathered everything of Nate's she could find. She stuffed everything she could into the suitcase he had left with her and threw it outside.

She slammed the door behind her, chaining and locking it before storming into her bedroom. She also closed and locked her bedroom door before sliding to the floor and beginning to cry. She had sensed the end coming, but she never expected to be the one to initiate it. Suddenly she realized that the necklace Charli had given her was still securely around her neck. She reached up to grab it and tear it off, then paused, remembering what Charli had told her: "It means happiness dear, and you deserve happiness." Instead of throwing the necklace away with Nate, Jen clutched it tightly. She willed its magic powers to work faster as she sobbed with increasing fervor.

She continued to cry for what seemed like hours until eventually, there was a knock at her door. She looked at the clock next to her bed and realized she had been bawling since midnight. It was now 2 am. There was another knock at the door, and then her phone began to ring. It was Nate. She let it go to voicemail. As soon as it did, he began to call again. This time, Jen answered.

"What? I think I made myself clear. Take your shit and get out." Jen spat into the receiver.

"Are you serious, right now? What in the hell happened? Let me in. Let's talk about this calmly and rationally, Jen." Nate begged as he gently knocked on the door again.

"No, Nathan. No. You lied to me tonight, and you were with another woman. I heard her when you answered and left the line open before hanging up on me. I told you I didn't care as long as it stayed behind when you came back for me after training. This infidelity isn't training, Nate. This infidelity is my home town. Go be with someone else for all I care." Jen yelled.

"What the hell are you saying? I wasn't with another woman. I didn't hear my phone. I left it in my coat pocket and hung my coat up. We were playing pool." Nate argued.

"Don't lie to me, Nathan. Just don't. Just go." Jen said once again as her voice cracked, and she began to sob.

"Jen... Okay. Okay. If that's what you want. I'll take my shit and go." Nate huffed quietly.

"Goodbye, Nate." Jen sobbed.

Nate didn't reply. He hung up the phone and gathered his suitcase and few other belongings Jen had tossed into the hallway. Nate got what he wanted. The relationship was over, and he was free to pursue Molly to any extent he wanted, but the rejection from Jen still stung. The longer he stood at her door, the more it began to eat at him until he dropped his things and slammed his fist into the steel security door.

"Fucking, bitch!" He yelled as he punched the door once more.

His hand throbbed from the impact, and Jen ignored his outburst. He briefly stood at the door, hoping that she would answer and confront him. Eventually, when the hall remained silent, and he could hear no movement from inside the apartment, he gathered his things and finally walked away.

After the breakup, Jen ended the lease at her apartment, quit her job, and moved far away. She wanted a new lease on life, and everywhere she looked back home, she had to endure constant reminders of Nate. Jen took a job with better hours and better pay. Things seemed to be going reasonably well all things considered, but she was still severely wounded from the breakup.

To ease the transition into single life once again, she rented a house with several other young women whom she had connected with through work. They had a lot in common, all being young adults in different transitions in their life. Lindsey had just begun a new relationship. Chelsea had lost her job. Amanda, like Jen, ended a long term relationship. They were all moving forward in their ways and enjoyed each other's company for the most part.

Jen cherished the necklace and rarely took it off after she ended the relationship with Nate. Just as she initially suspected, as soon as he returned home from basic training, he was already engaged to someone else, and she was pregnant. They had spoken a few times after the night Jen kicked him out to exchange a few belongings. The more space and time between herself and Nate grew, the more she realized how horrible the relationship had been all together. Jen finally saw Nate's abusive nature for what it was and realized that he never treated her well. While she tried to be civil during their necessary interactions, Nate was anything but polite.

Jen knew that Nate had a dark side. She'd seen it surface during their relationship, but it had never focused on her until now. It was overwhelming at times. Jen was trapped trying to grieve the loss of the connection and trying to wrap her head around how Nate could go from her boyfriend, one moment to her worst enemy the next.

Realizing Nate's true nature made the necklace Charli gave her so much more sentimental. While everything she knew about Nate turned upside down when the relationship ended, she could trust her assessment of his family. Charli and Wes genuinely cared for her, and in the middle of the pain and uncertainty, Jen clung to the hope that the charm would indeed bring her happiness.

One afternoon Jen was leaving a very hectic shift at the office. She was behind on her quota for the month, she had been putting in every extra available hour to make up for it, and the sales were not coming in. She was stressed, she was exhausted, and she bumped into Connor McAlister, stepping out of the elevator.

"Oh! I'm so sorry. I didn't see you there. I'm so sorry." Jen stammered as the stack of files she was carrying flew from her hands and scattered across the floor.

"No. No, I'm sorry. Are you okay? Can I help you?" Connor asked as he knelt and began picking up some of the scattered papers.

"Thank you. You don't have to." Jen said, also kneeling to retrieve her disheveled portfolio.

She reached just a hair too far to the left to pick up a sales report and tumbled over. That was the last straw for the day. Tripping in front of the man who stopped at the office was too much. As soon as she lost her balance and hit the floor, she began to sob, despite her best efforts not to.

"Seriously, are you okay? What's wrong? I know I'm just a random guy on the elevator, but you seem upset. Do you want to talk about it?" Connor offered, plopping down on the floor next to Jen.

"I… I don't know. I need to cry it out, I think." Jen squeaked between heaving breathes.

"Okay. I'll wait here with you. Your portfolio won't go anywhere. Ruthie isn't scheduled to arrive for another hour or two." Connor observed, glancing at his wristwatch.

"Ruthie?" Jen asked with a sniffle.

"Yes. Ruthie, she's the custodian who cleans the halls at night after everyone else usually goes home. I only know her, because I'm here often after most 'normal' business hours." Connor answered. "I'm Connor, by the way. Connor McAlister. I work at VyhoTech. Suite 603. I don't think I've seen you here before."

"Jen Smith. Jinks Marketing. Suite 610. Hi, neighbor." Jen sniffled as her tears finally began to subside. "I just started a few months ago. I haven't been here all that much. I mostly work from home."

"Me too. People suck." Connor lamented with a smile.

"Yeah. People do." Jen chuckled. "Present company

excluded."

"Oh, well. It's not every day you bump into a cute girl on the elevator on the way to the office."

Jen's cheeks flushed. It had been months since she'd felt this way. She wasn't sure what to do with herself. Nate had been her first long term relationship. When it ended, she was lost. Meeting Connor stirred something inside of her that she'd never felt before. Even with Nate.

"I'm sorry. Was that too forward of me?" Connor asked, noticing how uncomfortable Jen had become.

"Not at all, Connor. I... well, I'm just getting out of a long term relationship, and I'm not sure how to navigate the dating waters anymore." Jen answered, honestly.

"Really? Well, I just finalized my divorce yesterday. We've been separated for a while now, but the paperwork just went through. I'm a bit out of practice myself." Connor shared.

"Wow. I'm sorry. That's awful." Jen gasped.

"Yeah... What about you?" Connor asked.

"Nate was cheating on me. He was abusive too, but catching him with another woman was the last straw. I kicked him out." Jen sighed.

Connor grimaced.

"Small world full of assholes, huh?"

"I guess so."

The two sat quietly suddenly lost in their thoughts until the elevator dinged, signaling the doors would be opening soon. At that, they both scrambled to gather Jen's runaway papers before the doors opened.

"Well, Ruthie is here, so I guess I better be getting into the office now. It was a pleasure meeting you, Jen. Can I call you sometime? We can continue our conversation under better circumstances. Maybe dinner?" Connor offered while handing Jen the last of her portfolio as he stood and helped her to her feet.

"Sure. I'd like that." Jen answered as she carefully tucked

her documents back into her portfolio and pulled out her phone.

Connor proceeded to walk Jen to her car, open her door, and see that she was safely on her way before returning to the office upstairs. She was smitten, although practical. Both she and Connor just ended long term relationships. Jen wasn't entirely sure she was ready to date with everything else on her plate. But he was handsome, polite, single, and courteous. How often was she going to run into someone like that in the current dating scene? The answer was slim to none.

She pulled up to an intersection and let her hair down at a red light. When she did, it fell gracefully across her shoulders. As she went to brush the rogue strands behind her ear, something snagged against her neck. Almost by reflex, she instinctively grabbed for the pendant on her necklace. It felt warm to the touch after being securely draped around her neck for the day. She freed her hair from the chain and continued to stroke each line of the Kanji character as the light changed from red to green, and she made her way home.

A few days later, Jen peered at herself in the slowly clearing fog of the bathroom mirror. She stepped out of the shower and was getting ready to meet Connor for a late lunch date. While Jen had been excited to set up the date when they first bumped into one another, now she was apprehensive and unsure of herself. She looked at her tired eyes, and the lines worn into her face from grief and stress. Jen smiled and noted her crooked teeth, which seemed to be moving farther out of alignment every day. Her slightly damp hair frizzed the moment she touched it with a wide-tooth comb, and it didn't seem to matter how many products she used or didn't use beforehand.

She sighed and scowled as the hurtful words Nate would often utter filtered through her head: 'I wish you would do

something with your hair. I wish you wouldn't wear so much makeup. I wish you wouldn't wear that outfit...'
Thinking about Nate's hurtful words, tears began to well up in her eyes, and she had to turn away from the mirror.

She glanced at her phone, sitting on the vanity and slowly reached for it. She quickly accessed her contacts and briefly considered dialing Connor's number to cancel the date. They had spoken via text almost daily since they bumped into one another. Jen had no reason to think poorly of Connor. Still, the lingering words Nate left behind crawled in her ear like a parasite, and her hands shook as she hovered over the send call button.

Before she could decide, the phone began to ring in her hand, and the display lit up announcing that it was Connor. Jen jolted and nearly tossed the phone across the small bathroom, before regaining her composure and answering.

"Hello?" She answered timidly.

"Hi, Jen. It's Connor. I just wanted to let you know I'm going to be running a few minutes late. Is that okay?" Connor asked, hopefully.

"Sure. I'm just getting out of the shower. No rush." Jen answered as her heart rate began to slow.

"Okay, great. I'm sorry. My car is giving me hell. I finally got it started, but now it's rush hour, and you know how that goes. I didn't want you to think I had forgotten or something." Connor explained with a sigh of relief.

"It's no problem. I'm just glad I won't be holding up our evening. Living in a house with one bathroom and six women is a challenge, to say the least." Jen chuckled.

"Oh, wow. Yeah, that does sound like a lot. Okay, well, I'll be there as soon as I can get there. Hopefully, this traffic clears up. I'll see you soon." Connor explained before ending the call.

Jen took the handset away from her ear and stared at it. She felt her face grow hot with embarrassment and excitement, and she quickly applied her makeup and finished her hair before slipping into her favorite sundress. When she gathered her towel and other belongings to leave the bathroom, she looked at herself in the mirror once again. This time, she smiled.

Jen bounced across the hallway into her bedroom to stow her shower caddy and put on some jewelry to complete her look. She opened her jewelry box and stared blankly. She owned many jewelry items, but none that were very suitable for the occasion except the necklace and a set of earrings that Charli had previously given her for her birthday.

She gently took the earrings out of their designated spot and held them in her palm. While she loved them, she wasn't sure she wanted to wear them. Much like the necklace, Charli had given them to her as a token of good fortune, and it felt somehow inappropriate to keep them after the relationship with Nate went south. Maybe she would wear the jewelry just this one last time. It was her first date with Connor after all, and she felt like she could use all the luck in the world.

Once Jen shored her resolve, she placed the earrings through her lobes and secured the necklace around her neck. As soon as the clasp closed on the chain, a cold draft blew through the room. Something about it was comforting. Jen noticed that she often got chills, or encountered a draft after putting the necklace on. Still, she never considered the idea that the Kami associated with her jewelry caused these events. She just attributed it to low blood sugar or drafty old windows.

"Jen! Your man friend is here!" Lindsey called from the living room.

"Coming!" Jen answered as she shut her jewelry box, grabbed her purse, and headed out into the living room.

The house they were renting was an old cookie-cutter style house from the late fifties. It offered three small bedrooms, an eat-in kitchen, and one large living room with a picture window peering out into the neighborhood. The tiny basement, partially finished before they entered the lease, gave them a little bit more room for guests and social activities, but otherwise, it was pretty tight quarters. Jen didn't mind sharing the small space with her roommates, although she longed for the privacy of her own home again.

She walked into the living room and found Connor waiting patiently by the front door. As soon as she walked into his line of sight, his face lit up with a perfect smile, and his cheeks flushed slightly. Jen also smiled broadly and did her best to hide the flush she could feel growing across her face.

"You look amazing." Connor wowed quietly.

"Thank you," Jen replied, avoiding eye contact and staring at her shoes.

"Alright, you two. Save it for later. Go get some dinner and get out of here." Lindsey laughed as she left the living room and wandered into the kitchen.

Jen smiled again as she finally raised her head and looked into Connor's captivating green eyes.

"Shall we?" Connor asked, extending his arm for Jen to take hold.

"We shall," Jen answered, taking Connor's arm as they made their way out the front door.

They stepped outside, and Jen turned to close the front door. She inserted her key, and the lock tumbled with an audible snap before she turned around to take Connor's arm once again. They stepped off the porch and met a literal whirlwind as leftover dry leaves from the previous season swirled around them.

"What are you, a princess, or something with your swirling leaves?" Connor laughed as he batted a few rogue leaves away from his face and shielded Jen from them as well until the mysterious breeze finally subsided.

"If I'm a princess, you must be my prince charming," Jen responded. "Let's go find out."

With that, Connor threw his head back in a sincere and genuine laugh, and the pair climbed into Connor's car to head off to dinner.

Jen and Connor spent the evening together in the pure bliss of excitement and a new relationship. The restaurant Connor chose for their dinner provided excellent service, and the food was delicious. They sat together engrossed in conversation until they were the only patrons left and their server gently informed them that it was time to go.

After leaving the restaurant instead of heading straight home, Connor took Jen to one of his favorite spots downtown. It was a beautifully lit canal hidden below the bustling streets. Jen had visited the park at the mouth of the canal but had never ventured down to the canal itself. They walked hand in hand, enjoying the warm summer breeze that wafted around them, talking about everything and nothing.

As the night wore on, it slowly turned into moring. The sky went from a deep purple blanket with a pinprick star pattern to a dull orange glow as the sun began to peek over the horizon.

"Oh. Is it daylight already?" Jen asked, looking past Connor's captivating eyes for the first time that night and into the steadily warming horizon.

Connor glanced at his wristwatch.

"Wow, yes, it is. I'm sorry I kept you out so late." Connor apologized.

"No, no, it's okay. I'm having a wonderful time. Who needs sleep anyway, right?" Jen laughed.

"I mean, I guess sleep can be overrated, but I do enjoy it." Connor laughed.

"True…" Jen trailed off. "I guess we should be heading home. Thank you so much for the beautiful evening, Connor. I'm so glad I had the opportunity to come out with you tonight."

"I'm glad I had the opportunity to spend time with you too. We should do it again sometime."

"I'd like that. I really would."

The pair sat on the small park bench staring into one another's eyes for a few moments more. Then they quietly stood and walked back to the car as if they had been walking together for eternity.

One date turned into two, and then three. Before long, Jen and Connor settled into the patterns of a new relationship. Things were so different in the relationship with Connor, compared to the relationship with Nate, that Jen sometimes had a difficult time accepting it was real. They had been taking things at a nice slow pace, which was refreshing compared to Nate's frequent mood swings and desire to achieve instant gratification. Summer gave way to fall, and after several months of dating bliss, the time had come for Jen to renew her lease.

Connor never pressured her in regards to their relationship, but he did suggest that she move in with him as her lease drew to a close. He was very supportive and gave her ample room to decide what she wanted to do. He was waiting for her answer nearly two weeks, and as Jen stared into her morning cup of coffee sitting at her desk, she still wasn't sure what she wanted to do.

As if he could sense her thinking about the situation, her phone display lit up with a message from Connor. She reached for her phone and opened up the news to see a flurry of heart emoticons and sweet "just because" message. She immediately smiled, and her anxiety briefly waned. She responded to his message with her flurry of heart emoticons. They made plans to meet in the small restaurant on the first floor of their building for lunch.

Jen glanced at the small clock occupying the bottom right corner of her desktop. It was down to the wire. She had an hour and a half to make up her mind about moving in with Connor. As she was looking at the clock, she suddenly noticed a chat window blinking for her attention and realized that she was distracted for over an hour.

"Oops." She muttered under her breath as she straightened up in her chair and refocused on her work.

She spent the next two hours deeply engrossed in her job and barely noticed when the lunch notification popped up behind the rest of her work. It wasn't until her phone began to buzz with Connor's concerned notifications that she looked up at the time. As soon as she noticed, she quickly logged out of her work and picked up her phone to call Connor.

"Hi, Sweetie. I'm sorry. I got distracted by my project. I'm on my way. You can order for me. You know what I like." Jen reassured Connor over the phone as she quickly threw on her light jacket and headed down the stairs toward the restaurant.

The restaurant was almost impossible to get into during lunch hour. The food was delicious, and the prices were fair. As Jen squeezed her way into the busy lunch center, she quickly found Connor sitting at their favorite table toward the back of the dining area in a quiet corner.

"Hi, honey. You got me the strawberry salad! Thank you. That looks great." Jen said, wrapping her arms around Connor, who stood to greet her and giving him a quick peck on the cheek.

"I grabbed the last one. I'm surprised there were any left today." Connor answered with a smile as they both took their seats and began to eat their lunch.

Most of the meal they sat in silence, merely content to be with one another in the same space. Jen loved that about Connor the most. She didn't feel obligated or trapped in a conversation with him. He understood the value of silence without becoming insecure or restless. It was refreshing and comforting.

As the meal drew to a close, their conversation began to

flourish.

"Have you decided what you're going to do about your lease?" Connor asked as he gathered his napkin and other leftovers onto his plate.

"I… I've been thinking about it a lot. It's not you at all — I kind of like my independence. Living with Nate was so suffocating. It's been nice to breathe a little bit." Jen answered, honestly.

"It's okay, honey. I understand. We can wait. I don't want to rush you at all." Connor answered with genuine care and concern in his voice.

"I know. I appreciate that. I mean, don't get me wrong it would be nice to live with you and save some money on rent. My roommates are starting to get on my nerves, throwing parties every weekend and leaving the mess for me to clean up during the week. I guess I'm just scared. Nate is still harassing me, and I don't want to drag you into that shit show if I can help it." Jen explained, also taking the time to gather her leftovers and set them neatly on her plate.

"I think that's a great reason for you to move in with me. With your roommates being less than responsible right now, you're very vulnerable at the house by yourself. Nate sounds dangerous. At least if he tries something at my place, you won't be alone." Connor suggested.

Jen grimaced.

"I don't think he would go that far. He's mostly all talk." She replied, shaking her head as the thought of Nate filled her stomach with needles.

"I trust your decision. It's totally okay whatever you choose. We don't have to talk about it anymore. Are you okay?" Connor asked, noticing Jen's visible discomfort.

"Oh… well yeah. Pretty much. I'm just tired and distracted a lot this week. Work has been insane with the holidays approaching. Everyone wants their holiday marketing campaigns, and they want them NOW. "Jen lamented. "Things will slow down in a few weeks."

"I have some vacation time I need to use. Can I help with anything? Take a few days and clean up the mess at the house so you can take a break?" Connor suggested.

"Connor, that would be amazing. Thank you so much." Jen yelped as she jumped across the table and gave him a huge hug.

"Of course, Jenny. I'm always here to help." Connor answered, returning Jen's hug.

They embraced until each of their phones began to buzz with the unfortunate notification that lunch was over. They each collected their trash; then they joined the mass exodus of patrons heading back to their cubicles for the remainder of the workday.

Jen opened her eyes as the sun shone through the curtains and reflected off of her small vanity mirror. The house was quiet, which was a nice change for a Saturday morning. She crawled out of bed and opened her bedroom door to find the usual mess left behind by her roommates. She waded through trash and party supplies until she reached the bathroom.

"Well, that's nice, at least." She muttered, finding the bathroom vomit free this time around. "Connor can't get here soon enough."

Connor agreed to stay at the house for the week and help Jen clean up so she could relax and focus on her work. She was looking forward to having him there. She was also a little bit nervous since they had been dating for several months and had yet to move forward in their level of intimacy. She was terrified that by allowing Connor to stay at the house overnight, he would take advantage of her the same way Nate had before him. Connor and Nate were nothing alike, but still, the thought kept creeping into the forefront of her mind.

She splashed some cool water onto her face at the sink.

She made her way out to the living room where she occupied herself, attempting to pick up at least some of the trash and mess left behind by her roommates and their party friends the night before. Before she knew it, Connor knocked softly on the door.

Jen turned to answer it and wrapped her arms around him in a big hug.

"I'm so glad you're here." She said, squeezing him a little bit tighter.

"I'm glad to be here. Wow, you weren't kidding when you said your roommates were messy." Connor replied as he looked over Jen's shoulder to the mess behind her.

"They aren't messy so much, just the people they invite to their parties on the weekends," Jen said, allowing Connor to enter the house entirely.

He had a small duffle bag thrown over his shoulder and looked relaxed in a tee shirt and blue jeans. Jen had rarely seen him so casual since most of their dates occurred at or around their office schedules. She thought the casual style suited him better.

"Can I set this stuff in your room?" Connor asked, motioning toward his duffle bag.

"Sure. Of course. Here, this way." Jen answered, leading Connor back to her bedroom. Something she hadn't done since breaking up with Nate: leading a man to her bedroom. It felt awkward and a little bit uncomfortable. She hoped that he didn't notice.

"Here we are." She called as she opened the door to her room and wandered inside before plopping down in the middle of her bed.

Connor took stock of the small, yet neat bedroom that Jen called home. It was in direct contrast to the rest of the house. Her things, each of them kept in their place. The laundry neatly folded. What didn't fit in the laundry baskets was stored in a dresser and the closet. She kept a small wastebasket next to her vanity, which also dubbed as a writing desk. Any trash she might have acquired throughout the week was stored neatly in the basket. Her bed made, and the curtains were held open with smart clips; it looked like she fashioned out of hair ties and paperclips.

"What's wrong?" Jen asked, breaking Connor's train of thought.

"Nothing, honey. I was admiring your little space here. I like it." Connor answered, tossing his duffle bag in front of the small dresser and jumping onto the bed next to Kesley.

"I've been anxiety cleaning all week," Jen said with a nervous laugh.

"How about we get that anxiety cleaning energy and put it to good use? Let's get this place cleaned up. Are your roommates even home?" Connor said, hopping up from the bed.

"I don't know. Where there any other cars in the driveway when you pulled up?" Jen answered honestly, also sliding off the bed and following Connor out to the living room.

"Not that I saw. Where did they all go? I sure hope none of them drove." Connor observed as he kicked several empty red plastic cups and beer bottles out of the hallway.

"Lindsey's boyfriend lives a few blocks across town. They might have moved to the party there. Sometimes our neighbor complains." Jen answered, digging out a trash bag from a large box and handing one to Connor before throwing one open for herself.

"Party city, I guess."

"Something like that."

Before long, the entire house was clean top to bottom. It wasn't just picked up, but it was clean. Connor helped Jen mop and vacuum where necessary. They did dishes, folded and sorted the laundry strewn about all over the basement next to the laundry room. The cleaning project took most of the day, and they finished the evening off by ordering pizza and watching a movie.

Soon the movie drew to a close, and the sun had long since set, leaving the cool fall air and the crisp night sky full of brightly shining stars. Jen sat up and stretched with an enthusiastic yawn.

"I guess we should be getting to bed, huh?" She asked nervously.

"It does appear to be nighttime, and with night often comes sleep," Connor answered with a smile. "I'll just get my bag so you can get settled in." He yawned as he stood up and stretched his stiff neck.

"Wait... I thought you were staying here this week?" Jen asked, suddenly on alert. Was Connor leaving? Why was he going? What happened?

"I am. I thought I was going to take the guest room downstairs?" Connor clarified, also a bit nervous at Jen's sudden flare of anxiety.

"Oh."

Each of them paused, unsure of what to do or say. There had been a miscommunication, but neither Connor nor Jen was sure how to correct it.

"Do you want me to take the guest room? I... well, I could share your bed if that's something you want to do. I didn't want to assume." Connor finally said, taking a moment to sit back on the couch and take Jen's hand.

At that, Jen melted into an emotional puddle of tears. All of her anxieties fell away, and her soul felt renewed as Connor held her until she calmed the sea of tears and began to sob instead softly.

"Yes, Connor. You can share my bed. I'd love that." Jen finally said as she looked up at her boyfriend.

"Are you sure? I'm so sorry. I didn't mean to scare you or anything by taking the guest's room. We just haven't discussed intimacy in our relationship yet. Given your history with Nate, I just assumed that you would bring it up when you were ready." Connor explained.

"Do you have any flaws? I mean, do you?" Jen laughed.

"You're entirely too perfect, and it's weird."

"I have a few flaws. Maybe." Connor answered with a broad smile.

"Hmm… maybe, but I haven't seen any yet. Come on. Let's go to bed." Jen said, taking Connor's hand and leading him to the bedroom.

They stepped inside, and Jen closed the door behind them, throwing the lock, which made a small click.

"I'm ready, Connor. I'm ready to be with you here tonight, and I'm ready to move in with you. I love you." Jen whispered in Connor's ear as they began to kiss and collapsed together on the bed.

"You're sure?" Connor asked, returning Jen's kiss. "I love you too."

"Absolutely."

6 GUTTERBALL

The rest of Connor's time at the house was spent helping Jen gather her few belongings and packing them into moving boxes. She didn't have a lot, but it still took a few days to get everything in order.

"I'll see you at home later, honey," Connor said, giving Jen a gentle kiss on the forehead. He scooped up two boxes from Jen's nearly empty room and made his way outside to the car.

"Love you," Jen called after him.

The only things remaining of her transitional life in the house were her nightstand and the jewelry box sitting dutifully on top of it.

She grabbed the jewelry box and sat down with it on the floor before she opened it. Hanging on its hook right where she left it, was the necklace. While she had worn it on their first date, she rarely did anymore. It felt weird to hold on to something from her past as she was beginning to build a new relationship with Connor. Of course, the gift wasn't from Nate himself. She'd gotten rid of anything he left when she moved out of her apartment, and yet she still felt guilty for wearing it anytime she was with Connor. Maybe it was time to part with it as she was starting over. She didn't want an ounce of Nate's toxic nature to follow her into her budding relationship with Connor.

As she held the necklace, trying to decide what she wanted to do with it, Lindsey suddenly burst into her room with puffy eyes and tear-stained cheeks.

"Oh. I didn't know you were still here. I'm sorry. I'm…" Larua stammered.

"What happened? Are you okay?" Jen asked, tossing the necklace back into the jewelry box and standing to embrace her friend.

"Brandon wasn't answering his phone, so I went over there to tell him about this cool concert coming up, and he was with her, Jen! HER!" Lindsey yelled as her tears began to flow again.

"What? With who?" Jen asked, taking Lindsey's sobs onto her shoulder.

"Samantha! He said he was over her! He said he was over her. How could he do this to me?!" Lindsey wailed.

Samantha was Brandon's ex-girlfriend. The ex-girlfriend that he had cheated on to begin his relationship with Lindsey. Jen honestly thought that it was quite fitting karma to have Brandon leave Lindsey for Samantha. Still, she hated to see her friend hurting regardless of her disagreements in lifestyle choices.

"I'm so sorry, Lindsey. Here. Sit down for a moment. Let's talk about it." Jen offered as they both sat down and leaned their backs against the wall.

"I mean, I heard rumors that he was still seeing her behind my back, but I didn't know he was sleeping with her. Is our relationship meaningless? Does he not even care? He told me he loved me, Jen. He told me I was different." Lindsey sobbed.

Jen scowled. She had never been a fan of Brandon, but to hear how he had taken advantage of Lindsey made her opinion of him sink even lower. It reminded her of Nate and the same way he treated her. As the painful memory of Nate crossed her mind, it was then that she knew what she needed to do.

"Lindsey, I want you to have something," Jen said, reaching over to the jewelry box and retrieving the necklace. "Here. It's Kanji. It means happiness, and I want you to have it. You deserve happiness. Don't let Brandon's bullshit damage your self-worth. He doesn't deserve you. You're awesome, and you deserve so much more. Keep this as a reminder of that." Jen explained as she handed the necklace to Lindsey.

"Oh. Wow. Thank you. Isn't this the necklace Nate's mom gave you? Are you sure?" Lindsey asked, drying her eyes again and taking the necklace.

"Yeah, but I'm starting over. I don't want to take anything that belongs to Nate or reminds me of Nate and his toxicity into my relationship with Connor. I'm sure. Maybe it will bring you the same good fortune that it's brought me over the past year." Jen reassured her friend. She stood up and gathered the remaining jewelry in the box and closed the lid before taking hold of the box and sliding it carefully into the small drawer of the nightstand.

"You're welcome to have my room too. I need to get going. Connor is expecting me. Call me later, and we'll go have lunch or something to talk about Brandon's stupidity more." Jen said, offering Lindsey her free hand and helping her off the floor.

"I'm going to miss you, Jenny," Lindsey said as she stood up and gave her friend one final hug.

"I'm going to miss you too! This year has been crazy." Jen said, returning Lindsey's hug as best she could with her hands full. "Call me. Lunch."

"You bet. I'll call you." Lindsey said as Jen left the room.

Lindsey followed behind her to open the front door as she wrestled her belongings into her small sedan. Lindsey stood on the porch and waved as she observed Jen back out of the driveway and turn down the street, heading to her new life.

Jen disappeared, and Lindsey went back into her room, where she locked the door behind her and collapsed so she could cry again. She looked at the necklace in her hand. It was a small sterling charm on a sterling chain. It looked weathered, worn, and less than impressive. She thought it was a kind gesture, but the sentimentality behind it all wasn't significant to her.

"I don't know when I'm ever going to wear this thing. It looks like it's been run over by a truck." Lindsey mused to herself as she rolled over onto her back in the middle of the empty room before licking her finger and trying to brighten the silver.

Instead of shining brightly, the silver turned dull and sticky. Lindsey scowled and rolled over to return to her room. Once there, she pulled out a small container of jewelry cleaner and cotton ball. Lindsey haphazardly dunked the necklace into the cleaning solution and swished it around. She didn't pay much attention to whether or not the cleaning solution was appropriate for silver. It seemed to work on all of her other jewelry, and she didn't see why it wouldn't work on the necklace. After swishing around in the solution, she pulled it out. She began to buff away a dull film that had developed across the entire surface of the necklace pendant chain and all.

Slowly the necklace began to shine, but it wasn't a naturally vibrant shine as it had issued before. The jewelry, now coated in oil, made it artificially shine while weakening the chain and integrity of the silver.

Lindsey held the necklace up to the light pleased with herself until Amanda wandered into the room.

"Girl, tell me about what Brandon did this time! I got your text, but I was driving." Amanda called as she burst into the room.

"He was with Samantha. He wouldn't answer his phone, so I went over there to tell him about the show this weekend, and there she was. Right there, naked in his bed lying across his chest. I freaked out. I threw things at them both and ran out of the house as fast as I could." Lindsey answered, setting the necklace down on her dresser.

"Shut up! No, she did not." Amanda gasped.

"Yeah. Yeah, she did. It was awful. Brandon tried to call me a few times since everything happened, and I'm ignoring him. I came home and caught Jen just before she left. She gave me that necklace you wanted. It's on my dresser." Lindsey explained, pointing toward the necklace. "I don't know that I'll ever wear it. You can have it if you want."

Amanda reached for the necklace and picked it up.

"Are you sure? This necklace is elegant. Do you know what it means?" Amanda asked as she carefully put the necklace around her neck and fastened the clasp.

"She said it means happiness or something. I don't know. I don't care. I only took it so you could have it." Lindsey said, flopping down onto her bed.

"It's an Omamori. It's a blessed charm. It doesn't just mean happiness in terms of the character inscribed on it. The Kami, or god, of happiness, is attracted to it. If a Shinto priest blessed it, it could bring you happiness." Amanda explained as she admired the necklace before placing it around her neck.

"I don't believe in all of that. Besides, it looks better on you anyway." Lindsey insisted, sitting up to admire the necklace hanging gracefully across Amanda's collar bones.

"Okay, as long as you're sure. It has to be given away. It's bad luck if it's stolen." Amanda said. "What are you doing tonight? Let's go out to Bangerz, that new club, and forget about Brandon. Sound fun?"

Lindsey considered what she would do if she didn't go out with Amanda. When she realized the answer would be to sit at home and binge watch sappy movies, she agreed.

"Sure. That sounds fun. Who's going?" Lindsey asked.

"It was going to be just Chelsea and me, but now you and maybe Bethany. It'll be a good time." Amanda answered, running her fingers through her hair.

"Okay, cool. I'll pull myself together and ride down with you. What time did you want to leave?" Lindsey asked.

"Probably around nine or so."

"Got it."

Amanda nodded and headed out of Lindsey's room and wandered down the hall to her own. She briefly paused at Jen's now empty room. It would be weird without Jen. She had been the one to initially sign the lease and invite everyone else to move in. In a way, it felt like they were intruding even when the contract renewed in their names. The house had been Jen's house before anyone else. When she left, it felt like she took a piece of the soul out of the house with her.

Amanda wasn't particularly religious, but she knew something was out there. Until she could figure out precisely what that something was, she wasn't taking any chances by disrespecting any different religion. She had been coveting Jen's necklace since they first met at the office. This necklace was the reason they sparked a conversation. Amanda was familiar with the Shinto religions and customs because her grandmother had immigrated from Japan when she was a young girl. She remembered the stories and passed them down in the traditional oral storytelling style.

Unfortunately, Amanda never knew the significance of the stories until her grandmother had passed away. By then, it was too late. Her mother had all but forgotten the stories from her youth, and there was only one that stuck with Amanda. When she graduated high school, Amanda spent a good deal of her time researching Japanese customs and cultural history. She was trying to piece together the stories she missed so much from her grandmother. She found a few things, but none were as detailed and vivid as the stories from her youth.

She looked again in her small vanity mirror and admired the necklace. It looked like it was slick with baby oil, and the metal was no longer issuing the internal glow that drew her attention to it around Jen's neck. Amanda briefly wondered if the necklace was fading and worn because it had was separate from Jen. Lindsey said the jewelry was a gift, and Amanda believed her, but something felt different when it was around her neck. It felt heavy, physically, and metaphysically.

She brought her hand up to hold the pendant between her fingers, and it felt cold and clammy as if some internal energy was beginning to fade.

"Maybe I should give this back to Jen next time I see her." Amanda wondered allowed.

Jen and Amanda had never been very close. It was true that they lived under the same roof for the past several months, but mostly they each kept to themselves. Lindsey and Chelsea were the social butterflies of the house. They were always arranging parties or outings, and talking up a storm, getting to know details about every single person inside the house at any given moment. Of course, Lindsey and Chelsea were also known to take this information and use it to their advantage, spreading gossip and hateful lies when it suited their agenda. Amanda and Jen kept to themselves. They both worked a respectable 9-5 at the office and kept their things organized and put together. They enjoyed going out to drink and socialize with the rest of their housemates, but it wasn't in their list of top priorities. Amanda would miss the comradery she shared with Jen.

Amanda let out a deep sigh and opened her small closet sifting through her wardrobe in search of something appropriate to wear out to the club. The weather was cool, but not quite cold. Coupled with the fact that alcohol made

Amanda flush, she wasn't sure whether to chose a late summer outfit or something from her winter selections.

As she continued to flip through her closet, she found her hand subconsciously went to the necklace, where her index finger traced the Kanji in careful and thoughtful strokes. She thought of the silver and contrasting black of the pendant as she flipped past an orange sweater, then again past a deep mustard yellow jacket. Finally, she settled on a silver v-neck sweater paired with black leggings and tan leather boots. It wasn't her most elegant outfit choice, but it was something warm and straightforward, and it would make her new jewelry pop.

She quickly changed into her outfit and sat down at her small vanity, where she promptly applied some basic makeup. She opened her disorganized jewelry box. She dug around until she found the smart black onyx earrings she wanted to pair with the necklace. She completed her ensemble, brushed her hair, and spritzed some body spray across her chest.

As she was walking out of the room to make sure Lindsey was ready to go, she caught a glimpse of herself in the mirror and smiled.

Bangerz was packed. Amanda, Lindsey, and the rest of their friends had managed to get in relatively quickly, but once the rest of the town showed up, it was challenging to move around. The girls ordered several drinks. They sat around a small table loudly, yelling at one another and denouncing the troubles they encountered with various men in their lives. Eventually, they decided to move to the dance floor.

Lindsey was the first to dive into the fray, followed closely by Chelsea and Amanda. Amanda hung back at the table, dutifully watching the drinks as she watched her friends mingle with others they quite literally bumped into on the dance floor. Amanda had chosen a gin and tonic for her beverage of choice that evening, and she quietly nursed it as her friends moved in a gaggle from one side of the dance floor to the other. Eventually, bored with people watching Amanda pulled out her phone and began to text anyone in her contacts list that might not be out at a bar or club.

It was Friday night, and for a young professional woman in her early twenties finding someone to text would be a difficult challenge. She continued to scroll through her phone while absentmindedly fidgeting with the necklace until she reached Jen's phone number.

"Hey," Amanda typed into her phone and then pressed send. "I heard you gave Lindsey the necklace. Are you sure you want to do that? I mean, Lindsey?" She sent immediately after without waiting for a response.

A few moments passed until her phone buzzed in her hand with a response.

"Yeah, I gave her the necklace. I thought like she could use it with the whole Brandon mess. What ate you up to?" Jen answered.

"Oh, nothing just at Bangerz watching Lindsey, Chelsea, and Amanda make fools of themselves. Lol." Amanda replied.

She stared at her phone, waiting for a response when none came, she tucked her phone back into her small purse and stood to stretch her legs. If there wasn't anyone to talk to, she might as well dance. She tossed cocktail napkins into each glass remaining at the table and pressed her way into the sea of bodies that seemed to pulse with the music. She closed her eyes and took a deep breath before raising her arms and letting herself go. As she did this, the clasp which held the necklace around her neck snapped, and it tumbled to the floor. Amanda never noticed.

The necklace lay on the floor for several moments until the chain tangled around a stiletto heel. It scuffed along the floor as the owner of the stiletto stumbled around in labored dizzy steps until the necklace dislodged and flew several feet. Once it landed again on the floor, it was trampled and kicked back and forth until it became lodged into the soft foam rubber bottom of a sheepskin boot. It remained there the duration of the night until the owner of the boot stumbled to the bathroom. They yanked the chain freeing the pendant from the boot and launched it across the room just underneath the bar. There it bounced with the bass beat of the music until the last call, and the patrons began to filter out for the evening.

"Lights up!" Nick called from behind the bar, as he and the other staff began to clean up for the night. "Cheese and crackers, this place gets more disgusting every night." He mumbled to himself as he pulled a push broom out from behind the bar and walked around to begin the nightly task of putting Humpty Dumpty back together again.

"Hey, boss, I found something. Look at this. It's a necklace. A little smashed after being on the floor all night, but someone will be back for this." Katie explained holding a badly scuffed and tarnished silver necklace up for Nick to examine.

"Eh, I'll toss it in the safe for a while. Thanks, Katie." Nick grumbled as he took the necklace and stuffed it into his shirt pocket.

They finished their cleaning duties, and Nick made his way to the small manager's office with each till from the bar's several registers balanced precariously on his arm. He entered the code to the safe and popped it open as he adjusted the records and prepared the nightly deposit. He was just about to close the safe when the bent over to pick up a rogue quarter, and the necklace fell to the ground.

"Almost forgot about you," Nick mumbled as he tossed the necklace into the safe, closed the door and turned off the lights.

Fall again turned into winter, and winter again turned into spring. The necklace sat at the back of the cash safe in the manager's office at Bangerz undisturbed. No one ever came back to claim it, and no one ever thought to look beyond the cash tills as they were completing their business for the day. It wasn't until Nick received the news that the bar would be closing that anyone gave it any thought.

Bangerz had been the most exclusive local club before Nick bought it two years previously. He thought he knew what he was doing, but as things began to sink in and employees began to stop showing up for work, he realized that running a bar wasn't as easy as it looked. Nick wanted to pay the staff a fair wage, but he also wanted to keep the prices of the drinks reasonable to keep patrons coming through the doors. Try as hard as he might; he could never achieve a balance between the two.

His servers were overworked and underpaid. His customers were underpaid at their jobs and unable to afford an increase in drink prices, so they went to the next place down the road. Bangerz was hemorrhaging money. Eventually, as much as he hated to admit it, it was time to toss in the towel and get a "real" job.

The last night for business drew to a close, and he pulled cash out of each till before dividing it between the team. There was no need to keep the money. His business loan was in default and would remain that way for some time until he could find gainful employment.

It would be difficult to transition back to working for someone else when he had spent two years making his hours and deciding his salary. He would miss the freedom and flexibility that came with owning his own business, that much was certain. He would also miss two of his most loyal staff members who were closing with him tonight. They had become like family over the whirlwind attempt to open and keep Bangerz running. It would be weird to see them leave tonight and shutter the doors for good.

"We're all finished, Nick," Katie said as she wandered into the office, followed by her sister Beth.

"Thanks, girls. Here. Think of it as a severance package." Nick said, handing Katie and Beth each a stack of twenty-dollar bills. "Good luck out there."

"Thanks, Nick. We loved our time here. I'm sorry it has to end." Katie said quietly, accepting the money and passing the second stack back to Beth. "Goodnight."

The two worn-out servers turned around and walked out the front door.

Nick watched them, made sure the door shut securely behind them, and then set about cleaning the very few personal items he kept in the store out of the office. He unfolded a small cardboard box and began cleaning as much as he could. He hadn't sold the building just yet, but with it sitting empty after the end of the shift until who knows when he didn't want anything personal or financial lingering.

Soon the box was filled past the brim with various financial reports, payroll documents, and random personal things he'd left behind for good luck. He started to walk out the door when suddenly he realized that he hadn't emptied the safe. He sat the box full of trinkets down on the small desk and punched in the code one last time.

The heavy door swung open and squeaked as it reached the end of its hinges. Nick bent down and pulled the remaining funds stacking them carefully on top of the box. He was about to close the door once and for all, when something sparkled and caught his eye.

At first, he thought it was probably just a latent coin and considered closing the door and leaving it behind. Then curiosity took over, and he decided to reach into the safe and see what he could pull out. He felt around blindly until his fingers caught on a tarnished silver necklace. He pulled it out and looked it over. As soon as he touched the metal, it seemed to glow with an interior light and surprisingly felt warm to the touch.

He brought the necklace closer to his face to inspect the

barely legible inscription scratched across its surface.

"Is that English? Or some design?" Nick mumbled to himself as he continued to examine the necklace. "Eh, it doesn't matter. I'll clean it up and give it to Allison. She could use something to cheer her up after this disaster."

He tossed the necklace in the box and made his way out of the building for good. He was sad to see it go and somewhat relieved that he no longer had to deal with it all at once. He'd never been particularly sentimental, but saying goodbye to one of his life long dreams was still tricky.

He made sure the door shut behind him, set the box down on the sidewalk beside him, and dug out a small but heavy chain and padlock. He wrapped the chain around the door handles and secured the lock giving the door one final test tug before scooping up his belongings and continuing to his car.

The drive home felt much longer than it had when he first opened Bangerz. The bar was downtown, and he lived about twenty minutes away in one of the more affluent suburbs. Allison, his wife, was a cosmetic surgeon with a private practice. Nick was ashamed that his wife brought in most of their income, but today it stung even more. He pulled into their large garage, grabbed the necklace, and dragged himself inside.

Allison was sound asleep upstairs. He had plenty of time to clean the necklace before she would begin to stir for the day. He tossed it onto the kitchen countertop as he rummaged around through the cabinets looking for the sterling polish. Eventually, he found it and sat down at the breakfast bar to see if he could salvage the necklace. He grabbed a roll of paper towels and made a placemat before he stretched the chain out to its full length. Then, he carefully applied the cleaning solution with a cotton swab. The work was tedious but rewarding as the oxidation slowly began to fade away, and the true beauty of the silver started to shine once again. As he reached the end of the chain, he began to focus on the pendant. The oxidation was so heavy he still couldn't tell what if anything was engraved.

He dabbed the solution, allowed it to sit, then wiped it away. He repeated this process many times until finally, an outline of bright silver began to poke through the dense crust of time. Dab, wait, wipe away. It was almost hypnotic as Nick continued the slow process. Finally, just as the sun began to rise over the horizon and Allison's alarm began to sound, Nick was finished.

"Huh, I wonder what that means?" Nick asked to himself as he snapped a picture of the Kanji on the pendant and began to clean up his mess.

Nick assumed the symbol was one for good luck or some similar sentiment as he thoroughly dried the necklace and trudged through the house and toward the stairs. He slowly climbed the staircase until he reached the landing where Allison was stepping out of the bathroom after her morning shower.

"There you are. I couldn't imagine where you would go after the last call. I was starting to worry." Allison said as she brushed past Nick.

"Yeah. I had to clean out the office a little bit before I came home. Here, this is for you." Nick said, following his wife into their bedroom and handing her the necklace.

"Oh! Nick, you shouldn't have. Where on Earth did you get the money for this thing?" Allison exclaimed, taking the necklace from Nick and looking at it with a quizzical expression.

"I found it in the back of the safe. It needed a good clean and polish, but it cleaned up pretty good. It's real silver. I don't know who lost it, but I thought you might like it." Nick answered, tossing his clothes that smelled of stale cigarettes and sweat into the small pile of laundry in the corner of the room and climbing into bed.

"Oh…. yes. It's lovely." Allison answered through a strained smile. "Sleep well, honey. I need to get ready for work."

Nick had already closed his eyes and soon drifted off to a deep, yet troubled sleep.

Allison wandered into the large walk-in closet that was accented with her vanity and began to get herself ready for the day. She tossed the necklace aside and pulled out her pearls. Pearls were pure yet elegant. Something that Allison strived for in her line of work. It was of utmost importance to display the ability to present one's self as a cosmetic surgeon so her clients would trust her.

That, combined with the fact that she had no idea what the Kanji inscribed meant, she was hesitant to wear the necklace. Nevermind the fact that Nick had found the jewelry in the back of his safe. There was no telling who had owned the chain before, where it came from, or how much it could even remotely be worth. She picked it up and examined it once again. She wasn't a jeweler in any capacity, but she did have an excellent eye for detail.

It was silver, and it appeared to have been well cared for at some point during its dubious history. Still, as far as a hallmark or indication of value, she couldn't see one. She did notice, however, that the clasp broke. It looked like it had snapped or torn from something.

She pulled a small jewelry repair kit from her vanity and quickly repaired the damaged clasp. As far as she could tell, it would be secure. To test her theory, she promptly pulled the chain around her neck and opened the clasp. It snapped shut, and she gently pulled on the chain. When she was confident that it would remain secure, she brought her hands behind her head to remove it.

"It looks great on you, Allison," Nick mumbled.

"I didn't notice you were standing there, Nick," Allison answered. She slowly took her hands away from the clasp and placed them on the vanity as she began to check her hair in the small mirror.

"Yeah, I want to sleep, but I can't. I'm going back

downstairs." Nick growled as he stumbled toward the bedroom door.

"Well… guess I'm wearing this today whether I want to or not." Allison mumbled under her breath.

Nick was a loving husband at the beginning of their marriage. He had a temper, but it wasn't anything that appeared devastating at first. Allison had just graduated high school when they first met, and Nick was an attractive older man. He lavished her with attention and purposed, not even two months after their first date. Allison was love struck. She agreed to a quick shotgun wedding, and so began her life of wedded hell.

Not even two days after their marriage finalized did she begin to see the real Nick. His lavish attention soon became an excuse to control everything Allison said and did. Before they got married, he agreed to pay for Allison's schooling as she continued her education. She thought it was a token of love and appreciation, but what it became was a bargaining chip. Any time she did something that he deemed unworthy, he would threaten to withdraw his bank account from her funding.

Soon the abuse evolved from merely controlling behavior to demeaning physical abuse. Nick never left a bruise where concerned friends or family might see, but the pain was just as real even when the wounds weren't visible to the general public. Somehow Allison managed to finish her education and become a successful doctor, but the abuse was not without its price.

Due to Nick's rampant infidelity, Allison contracted an irreversible STI. It left her unable to bear children. When she first received the news, she was heartbroken. As reality set in, she eventually became thankful that Nick would never be able to reproduce. At least with her.

The thought of leaving him had crossed her mind so many times in recent years as her practice finally became established, and yet she could never bring herself to do it.

Nick treated her poorly for sure, but he was full of insecurities himself. He was a sad, helpless little man, and right now, he didn't have a leg to stand on in terms of income. Now was finally her chance to transfer the mortgage and both cars into her name. Once that was over, she could file for divorce and kick him to the curb.

She had spent 20 hellish years with the man, and enough was enough. As she finished getting dressed and ready for the day, a genuine smile spread across her face. She quickly slipped downstairs and into the garage before Nick took notice, hopped into her car, and drove away to the freedom of her office.

The day wore on without much excitement. Allison made sure to tell a few people about the thoughtful gift Nick had given her so they would mention it the next time they saw him wander into the office. Then she directed all of her attention toward her patients. Allison had several consults, and several follow-ups on the books today. No surgeries, unfortunately, but she would make due. She didn't anticipate Nick to make a surprise visit since he got home so late last night, but she could never be too sure.

He would be calling her as soon as her office closed, wondering where she was and how much longer it would take her to get home. If she were even a few minutes late due to traffic, there would probably be a beating on the horizon for her. She momentarily shuddered at the thought of returning home to Nick before refocusing on the charts in hand. She hated that he had so much control over her, even amid her workday. Soon it would all be over. She couldn't wait.

As the day came to an end, the staff made their way out of the office for the evening. Allison lingered over some charts and referrals. Nick had been surprisingly silent all day. He hadn't stopped by for a visit, and he hadn't called her at all. She was somewhat relieved, but also apprehensive at his sudden change in behavior. She even called him several times and received no answer. She thought maybe he was with another woman. Yet, if he was, he usually answered the phone to keep up the poor facade of fidelity.

She absentmindedly stroked the necklace pendant as she mulled through the charts until her phone began to ring. She looked at the display and didn't immediately recognize the number that flashed across the caller ID. Puzzled, she answered with a reserved: "Hello? Dr. Hubble, can I help you?"

"Yes, ma'am. It's Detective Laurence with the Metropolitan Police Department. I have some news regarding the well being of your husband. Are you prepared to hear it?" The voice on the other end of the line explained calmly.

"I… Yes. I think so?" She answered as she held her breath.

"This afternoon, your neighbor reported hearing a gunshot come from your residence. We entered the home when no one answered the door and found your husband in the living room. He died of an apparent self-inflicted gunshot wound at some point earlier today." The detective explained. "I'm so sorry."

Allison sat stunned as her jaw dropped.

"My husband… is dead?" She sputtered.

"Yes, Ma'am. Are you okay?" The detective asked.

She wanted to jump up and dance on her desk. Still, considering the circumstances surrounding her husband's death and the secret she kept of his abuse, she thought better of it and merely answered: "Yes, I'm shocked. I had no idea. He just gave me a beautiful necklace early this morning. I can't believe it."

"We're going to need you to come to the scene and make an official statement, release the body to the coroner, and a few other formalities. Will you be able to do that?" The detective asked.

"Yes. I'll leave the office right now. It shouldn't take

more than twenty minutes for me to get home." Allison answered, quickly putting away paperwork and gathering her personal effects.

She rushed down the stairs of her small office building. She reached the front doors just as a tremendous thunderclap sounded across the sky, followed by a torrential downpour.

"Oh, great," Allison mumbled, trying to judge how long the rain would last and if she could make it across the parking lot to her car without completely ruining her smart wool suit pants.

She waited a few moments, and when she could see no visible sign of the downpour coming to a stop, she threw open the door, shielded her face from the rain, and ran as fast as she could until she reached her car. She was in such a hurry that she didn't notice the clasp on her necklace had come loose. The chain stayed dangled from her hair, but the pendant slowly slipped off and splashed into a small puddle by her feet.

As soon as she got to the car, she closed the door, started the engine, and quickly backed out of her parking space. When she did, she sent a wake of water sloshing through the puddle, which lifted the pendant off of the pavement and sent it sliding slowly down into the gutter.

7 FIRE AND WATER

The pendant tumbled along, snagging itself here and there on errant sticks and stones until it finally washed down into a storm drain. There it dropped in a free-fall until it splashed onto a leaf and began its journey through the sewer system. The leaf made an excellent boat as the pendant rode the turbulent stormwater deeper underneath the city. It traveled through several grates, filters, and tunnels until it splashed out into the open water of the river, which wound its way through the city.

As soon as it tumbled out of the sewer system and hit the churning water of the river below, its leaf boat immediately capsized. The current of the quickly swelling river carried the pendant downstream until it finally caught on the branch of a submerged tree where it remained, reflecting the moonlight like a lure.

The moonlight soon gave way to sunlight. The storm subsided, and the sun began to rise, sending its rays filtering through the muddy river water. The necklace remained firmly attached to the tree until a school of fish swam by. Several fishes took an interest in the shiny pendant, but only one was large enough to swallow it whole.

The pendant became lodged in the fish's mouth, where it remained for several days until the fish spotted something else shiny in the water and went to investigate. It opened it's mouth wide, and just as it was about to swim away, Lance yanked the line hard, hooking it.

The fish put up a good fight, but it was no match for Lance's fishing skills, and he slowly reeled it in.

Lance wasn't always a good fisherman. He used to be an influential stockbroker who thrived off the intense fluctuation of the market and constant gambling that came with his job. Lance was riding a wave of success as soon as he graduated from college. He married his high school sweetheart, and they had three healthy children. Their relationship strained with the amount of time Lance spent at work. Still, they made it work until Lance made a poor prediction of market trends and lost millions for his clients.

At first, it was only one client that abandoned him. Most f his clients remained loyal as he'd never steered them wrong before. Slowly, when Lance couldn't recover their investments, no matter how frantically he tried more and more of his clients jumped ship until there was no one left. Not only had he cost his clients millions, but he effectively severed any income for himself.

He tried his best to hide his failure from his wife, and for a few months, he was successful. Then the bill collectors started calling, the house went into foreclosure, and the cars became repossessed in the middle of the night. He couldn't hide it anymore, but it was too late. As soon as he explained to his wife that they were bankrupt, she packed up the kids and left him. He didn't have anything to offer her in the divorce, but it didn't matter. She found a small apartment for herself and the kids, and that was the end.

Lance lived in the house as long as he could and tried desperately to find another job. One thing after another fell through until he had nothing except the clothes on his back. After several months of staying with friends, he finally accepted his fate and made his way to the homeless shelter downtown. His wife found a job out of state and moved as soon as the divorce finalized. Lance was alone.

It had taken him a while to become accustomed to life on the streets. Eventually, he settled in and even began to enjoy himself. Living on the streets was a lot like playing the market. Everything was a gamble, and nothing was guaranteed. He often missed his family and especially his children, but he was overall content with his life. He spent the past fifteen years as a homeless nomad. He hadn't considered going back to his traditional lifestyle until he received a letter from his oldest daughter. She was getting married and wanted him to attend.

Ever since Lance received the letter, he had been trying to scrounge and save every cent he could find, for a plane ticket. He was surprised that his daughter would even consider inviting him since she hadn't seen him in over ten years. If there was one thing that would inspire him to return to a traditional lifestyle, it was his children.

As he pulled his dinner out of the river, he patted his breast pocket. Hidden under several shirts and his heavy winter coat was a small pouch of cold hard cash. It was quite a liability to keep it on his person. However, most banks frowned upon opening an account for a homeless person. He was about $100 short of the price of a ticket, and the wedding was in two weeks. He'd exhausted all of his resources and was at a loss.

He climbed back up the bank and wandered quietly down the street through the bustling pedestrian traffic. He ignored the ignorant and disgusted looks he received, accepting them as karmic retribution for the ignorance of his youth. He reasoned that he did look a little out of place carrying a fish down the street with his hair matted and unwashed layered in several different colors and styles of clothing.

He walked two more blocks before cutting down an

alleyway until he reached a large gate. The gate appeared locked to those merely passing by. In reality, it was the gateway to the homeless community where Lance was currently residing. They often joked about living in a gated community amongst themselves. They took up the ground floor of an abandon parking structure. The building attached to the parking structure was abandoned as well, but it was locked up tighter than Fort Knox. Many tried to get in but had been unsuccessful.

Lance liked the parking structure. It was out of the weather, but still open enough for the small fires necessary to keep warm and prepare some foods when available. You could light fires in abandon buildings, but then there was the risk of causing a structure fire and ending up in jail. Lance had managed to avoid incarceration over his life living in the homeless camps, and he intended to keep it that way. Many of his neighbors were addicts and participated in illegal activities to fuel their addiction. Lance tried to keep himself out of that part of the vagabond lifestyle.

He waved to two of his neighbors and sat down quietly in front of his dilapidated little home. It was pieced together out of cardboard boxes and a small nylon tent that someone lost from the top of their car one afternoon. It wasn't much, but it was home. He tossed the fish onto the floor of his small tent and began to gather the necessary equipment to prepare a cooking fire.

He sat down and crossed his legs in front of him. He slowly shredded small scraps of newspaper and cardboard, making a little pile inside of a metal baking pan he found behind a bakery. It wasn't the best way to contain his fire, but it was better than nothing. After he prepared his kindling, he took out his trusty lighter and lit a small section of the newspaper. The fire quickly took off as he added some small sticks and pieces of broken furniture he had collected from various dumpsters and trash cans around the block. Once the fire was self-sustained, he turned to the fish and pulled out a small pocket knife to gut and filet his meal.

After learning to survive on whatever he could catch in the river, he made quick work of the fish. He removed each fin and sliced it down the middle. As he turned it upside down in preparation to remove the skeletal sections, something fell into his lap. At first, he ignored it. It looked like a lure, but then a swift wind blew through the parking structure and nearly extinguished his hard-earned fire. He dropped the fish and stood to shield the flames. When he did, the pendant fell from his lap and clattered across the floor into view.

"What is that?" Lance mumbled to himself as the wind subsided, and he returned to his seat in front of the fire.

He scooped up the pendant and brought it close to his face squinting as he wiped mud and debris away to reveal the bright silver underneath.

"Is that silver?" He gasped. "Wow. How on Earth did you get inside this fish little trinket?"

Lance shook his head in disbelief. He quickly slipped the pendant safely inside his breast pocket close to his heart as he promptly finished preparing his meal. Lance wasn't sure how much his little trinket was worth, but it just might be enough to buy his ticket. He would investigate after lunch.

Lance stood, staring at his reflection in a bus stop shelter. The observation wasn't as precise as it would have been in a mirror, but it was the best he could do. He had shed several layers and attempted to wash himself up in a transit station bathroom. He still looked weathered and smelled awful, but at least he didn't look like he had crawled out of a dumpster anymore. He took a deep breath and turned to look at the massive gold and mahogany sign prominently attached to the front of a small jewelry shop.

Henry's Fine Jewelry would be the third store Lance had visited in as many hours. Each time he wandered into a store, the staff almost immediately asked him to leave. He tried to explain and even show them the pendant, but it never mattered. Henry's was his last hope before giving up on jewelry stores and heading to the local pawn shop. He knew he wouldn't get a fair price if he took it to a pawn shop, but if he couldn't even speak to someone at a jewelry store, pawning was his last option.

Steeling himself for immediate rejection, Lance opened the front door and stepped into Henry's. He met with a warm blast of air which startled him initially. Living outside in the elements for so long, Lance wasn't expecting warm air for at least several more weeks. He soon realized that Henry still had the heat on for the year and had to chuckle to himself.

When he wasn't run out of the shop, he slowly took several cautious steps toward the back where a cash register sat on a small display case. He was surprised how empty the store looked compared to the others he had visited just this morning. There were only three display cases, and each of them featured one specific kind of jewelry. There was a display for gold, for silver, and various materials other than gold or silver.

The rest of the shop was devoid of anything aside from well-kept hardwood floors that shone brightly and offered a stark contrast to the light grey walls. Lance looked around and then considered that Henry's might not be a legitimate jewelry business at all. He briefly wondered if it was a front for drugs or other nefarious activities. Suddenly an older man, bent over nearly half from age hobbled out of the back room and stopped at the register.

"Hello, welcome to Henry's. I'm Henry. How can I help you?" The older man asked, pushing glasses with thick bottle lenses up onto the bridge of his nose.

"Uh… hello. Yes, sir. I'm looking to see if you might be interested in purchasing a small pendant I have." Lance explained, as he took the last ten steps and finally reached the payment counter.

"I might be, let's see it," Henry answered, leaning onto the counter and setting his cane beside him.

Lance carefully pulled the pendant from his breast pocket and slid it across the counter.

Henry adjusted his glasses again and picked up the pendant.

"This is quite a trinket," Henry observed. "Where did you get it?"

"You wouldn't believe me if I told you. It's not stolen if that's what you're wondering." Lance answered.

"No, I know it's not stolen. If it were, it would still have the chain. I'm sure you found it. Do you live in the camp a few blocks west of here?" Henry asked, turning his attention away from the pendant and giving Lance a once over.

Lance wasn't used to being addressed as a homeless person so directly, yet politely at the same time.

"Uh… no actually. I'm over on Bernard St." He answered nervously.

"Hmm… What do you want for it? You aren't an addict of any kind, are you? Don't lie to me. I'll be able to tell if you lie to me." Henry asked as if he were a father speaking to his wayward teenage son.

"I'm not an addict. I need some money to buy a plane ticket. I'd like to see my daughter get married in two weeks, and maybe a shower and a shave." Lance answered, honestly.

"Mm…" Henry huffed, returning his attention to the pendant and carefully tracing each stroke of the Kanji with his index finger. "How about $150? Does that sound like it will help you?"

"That little thing is worth $150?!" Lance yelled in surprise.

"No. This thing is only worth about $45, but that's not what I asked." Henry replied.

Lance was beside himself. $150 was the exact amount he needed to get himself cleaned up and buy the ticket to his daughter's wedding, not a penny more nor a penny less. He never mentioned a dollar amount before, and he couldn't begin to imagine how Henry had come up with the exact number.

"Well... yes. That would be more than enough, but why? Why are you helping me when that isn't worth the money?" He finally answered.

"Some things are more important than money. You seem like a fairly honest fellow. I don't know what got you down on your luck, but I'd like to help. I'll write you up a sales ticket. Just a moment." Henry explained as he took his cane and slowly made his way to the back room with the pendant securely in his hand.

Henry sat the pendant on his workbench and slowly reached up to grab a small file box of old receipts. He shuffled around until he found the sheet of paper he was looking for, then pulled it out and scribbled something across the face. He then turned around and shuffled back out to the cash register and Lance, who was beginning to pace.

Henry slowly punched in each key on the cash register with deliberate intent, pausing to adjust his glasses several times until the drawer popped open with an audible ding. He then counted out ten individual twenty dollar bills, folded them, then wrapped them with the receipt in a small rubber band.

"There we go. Good luck to you, sir. I hope you make it to the wedding." He said with a smile as he handed the money to Lance.

"That's it? You don't need to see my ID or have a home address or..." Lance asked, hesitating before accepting the money.

"No. I need you to get out of here and get on your way to see your daughter. Here. Take it." Henry insisted, still smiling.

"Thank you. I don't know what else to say." Lance exclaimed, finally taking the money from Henry's outstretched hand.

"Just tell your daughter how to avoid the mistakes you made, so she doesn't end up in this situation, okay?" Henry said, outstretching his hand.

Lance took Henry's hand and delivered a firm handshake before turning around and walking back out into the sun. Lance had all the money he needed, and now he was going straight to the airport to buy a ticket. He would purchase a suit and get himself cleaned up once he arrived. It was the first time since he had decided to continue his vagabond lifestyle that his luck had turned around. He was overwhelmed with joy and couldn't wait to see his children again. Maybe, a traditional lifestyle wasn't so bad after all.

Henry smiled, watching Lance leave the shop. There wasn't much good left he could do battling stage 4 lung cancer, but what he could do was to help that young fellow turn his life around. At least Henry hoped that the young man would turn his life around after he had the opportunity to reunite with his daughter. Henry knew that if he could go back and do it all again, being able to see his child one more time would have made all the difference.

Henry started his small downtown jewelry store after he received a substantial inheritance from his father. He devoted all of his time and energy to the store. Often he was there from sun up to sun down and into the wee hours of the night. It was kind of amazing that he was able to start a family with his wife at all.

His wife, Lucille, had been supportive in the early stages of their relationship. But, as time wore on and Henry spent more and more time at the shop soon, Lucille became resentful. She began to flirt with the widower who moved in next door, and when Henry still didn't take notice, she eventually packed up the kids and left him. Of course, it was uncomfortable to live in such proximity to her ex-husband. After several months, Lucille finally convinced her new husband to move away from the city and out into the suburbs.

When Lucille moved, the children went with her and never had a prominent roll in their father's life again. Henry never took the time to foster a relationship with his children before or after the divorce. Now, as he was preparing to reach the end of his lifetime on Earth, he was entirely alone. He had spent the last five years doing his best to liquidate his inventory and clean up the shop. It wouldn't be long now until the disease would leave him incapacitated and in hospice care. He didn't need to take on another project piece, but hearing the young man filled with regret speak of his daughter's wedding, Henry couldn't help himself.

He stood at the counter a few moments lost in his thoughts before turning around and disappearing into the back room. He hobbled as fast as his failing legs would carry him and climbed up to his workbench to take a closer look at the pendant. He secured it onto his third-hand stand and adjusted his desk lamp until the pendant sparkled with what seemed to be an inner glow.

"Hmm… you are a special one, now aren't you?" Henry mumbled to himself as he turned the pendant side to side. "I wonder how old you are? Or where you originated? No hallmark that I can see. Must be handmade. It looks like you're missing your chain, little fella."

Henry slowly stood from his desk and walked a few feet until he reached a small cabinet filled with various supplies. He remembered putting a sterling chain aside from another project not too long ago; he would have to find it.

He shuffled through a few drawers and boxes of miscellaneous items until he found it. He carefully pulled it out and made his way back to the bench.

"Here we go, little fella. It's probably not as nice as the

one you had, but it's better than nothing. I'll have to solder you a new bale, but that shouldn't take too much time. We'll give you a nice bath too. It looks like you've been banged around quite a bit here recently." Henry mumbled quietly to the pendant.

His silver, gold, and precious stones were all he had left in this world. They would listen to him without judgment, and they, for the most part, would behave when he asked them to bend or sparkle in a certain way. It was a lonely existence, yet a peaceful one.

Henry pulled out a buffing cloth and cleaning solution. He carefully cleaned the pendant and prepared it for soldering. Henry decided that instead of creating an entirely new bale, he would merely cut and repair the existing one. Sterling was a soft metal, and he should be capable of snipping right through the bale to attach it to its new chain.

He pulled his trusty silver snips out of their home at the left corner of his desk, steadied the pendant, and adjusted his glasses. His hands shook as he struggled to grab ahold of the snips and bring them close to the bale. As soon as he made contact with the metal, his hands instantly became steady and carefully sliced right through the bale. Once it was cut, he used a pair of tweezers to carefully pry the metal apart just enough for the delicate link in the chain to pass through. As soon as the chain passed through the bale, he pinched it closed with tweezers and set down his other tools in favor of his soldering iron and a sliver of silver solder.

The smoke rose from the solder as it liquified in an intricate tendril. Henry loved the scent of soldering. The only process more pleasing he had found over the years was forging an entirely new piece from scratch. He would miss the scent of soldering the most. He removed the iron from the solder. He allowed it to cool before tossing the entire thing into a cooling flux solution.

The carbon coating left behind by the heat cracked and

repelled from the silver as a small puff of steam lifted from the solution. Henry smiled as he pulled the piece from the solution and dried it with a polishing cloth. The pendant shone as if it infused with a new life.

"That's better little fella. You look like a million bucks again. Amazing. Amazing. Whoever made you took a great deal of pride in their work. I'm glad I had the opportunity to work on you and bring you back to life. I can't say where you'll end up when I go, but I hope you bring someone else as much joy as you've brought me in the twilight of my life." Henry quipped as he held the pendant, now at home on a delicate silver bracelet above his head. He watched the light from his small desk lamp reflect and refract, sending small beacons across the workshop.

If Henry didn't know better, he could have sworn the pendant sparkled a little bit brighter as he spoke to it. Henry didn't particularly believe in magic, but at this stage of his life, he was starting to wonder. Anything seemed possible as he leaned heavily on his cane and made his way to the front of the shop and set the bracelet carefully into the most prominent display case.

He smiled as he closed the display case and returned to his workbench, leaving the bracelet behind.

The day wore on with a few customers wandering into the shop, but eventually, it was time to close and call it a day. Henry carefully put each item from the display cases securely into his time-locked safe. He locked the front door before heading out back to his car, faithfully waiting in the alley behind the shop. He groaned as he slid into the driver's seat and struggled to buckle his seat belt. His chest felt heavy and painful. His cancer was getting more difficult to ignore as each long day wore on. He knew the days he had left on Earth slowly drew to a close, and yet he continued with his daily duties mostly as if nothing was wrong. He could feel his body slowly losing strength. It wouldn't be much longer until the physical limitations of his disease would render his iron-will irrelevant.

He started the car and turned on the headlights before shifting into drive and pulling out into the quiet downtown streets. He kept the shop open just long enough to avoid most of the rush hour traffic. By the time he was ready to go home, downtown was silent after rush hour and before the nightlife began to take over.

He only lived a few blocks away from the shop in a rundown old brownstone that had been neglected by the gentrification committees. His neighbors were good people, and like him, most of them had lived in the neighborhood their entire lives. He couldn't imagine what would happen to the place after his death. He didn't leave anything to his children. He didn't leave anything to anyone. As far as Henry was concerned, he was alone in life and wouldn't need anything after he died. He wasn't sure what would happen to it all, but he wouldn't be taking it with him.

Most of his belongings he had given away to various friends or customers, much like the young man who came in down on his luck. All that remained in his sprawling home was a small television, microwave, and worn old recliner. He had long accepted that he could no longer climb the stairs to his bedroom. Most of his life remained in the car or the living room. It was challenging enough to climb the small iron staircase to his front door.

He pulled to a stop in front of his home and slowly climbed out of the car. Clinging to his cane, he struggled up the stairs until he reached the front door and unlocked it. Once he was inside, he tossed his keys on the barren sideboard. He shuffled into the living room, where he collapsed into his chair and reached for the television remote.

He was hungry, but he was too tired to prepare anything to eat. Skipping one meal wouldn't kill him any faster than cancer. He flipped through the channel roster once completely and began over again. Nothing grabbed his attention. The pain in his chest began to grow, and it became harder to breathe each time he clicked through to the next channel. Finally, the remote fell from his hand, and he closed his eyes. He took several more labored breathes; then, he went forward into the afterlife.

8 FORGOTTEN WARS

"I don't know what the code is. Dad never told us." Bridget, Henry's oldest daughter, complained into her cell phone as she sat frustrated in front of the safe at the shop.

Her father remained in his chair for two weeks until the next-door neighbor noticed his car hadn't moved, and the shop hadn't opened. It took an additional month to track down his children and sort out debts and other belongings. Bridget was assigned the arduous task of figuring it all out. Her younger brothers didn't want to be bothered with it, and their mother was in too frail of health to care.

So now, she sat in the middle of the dark and empty forlorn store, trying to figure out how to access the inventory left inside the safe. It was the only thing that she hadn't been able to liquidate. Everything else was long gone. All that remained of her father was the sign outside the building, and whatever remained in the safe.

"I don't know how you can verify that I am who I say I am. Can't you send someone down here to see that I haven't broken into the store?" Bridget argued.

She had been on the phone with the safe company trying to figure out how to access the contents for several hours. She was losing her patience.

"Well now, if I was a criminal, why would I be asking you how to get into the safe? That doesn't make any sense, and I don't appreciate your accusations. I'm about to throw the damn thing off the bridge into the river and call it done. There is nothing you can do?" She huffed as she kicked the door to the safe. "Fine. Whatever."

She hung up the phone and kicked the safe again. Her foot ached to remind her that she wasn't invincible and calmed her temper momentarily.

"Where the hell did you put the code to the safe, dad?" She hissed under her breath as she rubbed her forehead, trying to think of any place she might have neglected to look.

Having no other alternative, she began to look at every scrap of paper left in her father's desk, cash register, and workbench. She found many numbers, but none of them was the combination to the safe. She had tried them all several times. Finally, as she stared at the safe, mentally willing the door to open, a thought occurred to her. The safe was free-standing. Instead of trying to sort out the contents of the safe to send to auction, she could auction off the entire safe.

"Ugh, why didn't I think of that before?" She chastised herself as she pulled out her phone and called a moving company.

Soon the safe and it's contents were listed at a prominent estate auction house where Pearl and Norm had been watching it closely. No one else seemed to take much interest, which for them was a fortunate thing. Norm had just retired, and they both decided to rent a booth at the local antique mall. They didn't have many antiques themselves, but they had a decent chunk of money to get started. The safe was the most expensive thing they'd ever bid on, and the auction was only the third auction in which either of them had participated. Peal had a natural knack for all items of value. As soon as she saw it and read the description card that came with it, she knew it would be the best investment for their money.

Norm trusted her instinct. After being married for close to sixty years, he learned that when Pearl "had a feeling," you shouldn't argue with her. So far, Pearl's instinct had never been wrong. He didn't see why he should doubt her this time, which left them waiting not so patiently in the auction hall for the bidding to start.

"I have a good feeling about this safe, Norm." Pearl shared excitedly from the hard folding chair next to her husband.

"Yes, dear. I know you do. I hope that intuition of yours is still on the mark. It's a lot of money to invest in something we can't sell later. They don't even have the combination for it, and we don't even know what's inside of it. For all we know, it could be empty, and then what are we going to do with it?" Norm replied, factually. "Especially if we have to damage it to get into the thing. It will be worthless to everyone then."

Peal harumphed toward Norm. Her intuition was never wrong. She had been around for almost ninety years and not once had it ever led her astray. There was something she was meant to have inside of that safe. She could feel it in her old bones. It was important. The logistics of getting it open or selling off whatever might be inside of it after the fact was boring and trivial as far as she was concerned.

The auctioneer arrived on the stage and curtailed the rest of their argument. Pearl sat on the literal edge of her seat, waiting for the safe to arrive on the stage. She had her number placard firmly in hand, and her palms were beginning to sweat. Pearl loved the rush that bidding on a live auction brought. She didn't get out much after she quit her job at the bakery, which is why she wanted to help Norm with the booth. Antiques had always been his hobby, and she hadn't paid much attention until recently.

"Oh!" She nearly squealed involuntarily as she safe was wheeled out onto the stage.

"The next item up for bid is this SafeMaster 7000, and it's contents removed from a local jewelry store after the inventory liquidation. We do NOT have the access code. We'll start the bidding at $5,000. Do I have $5,000?" The auctioneer droned on.

Pearl excitedly raised her number high over her head.

"Alright, the first bid of $5,000 is on the books. Do I hear $5,500?" The auctioneer continued.

Peal looked straight ahead, willing the safe to almost jump into her possession arm and placard extended straight as an arrow.

"$5,500." A voice called from behind them.

"Trying to make it interesting, are you?" Peal muttered under her breath to her invisible adversary. "$7500" She called loudly.

"$7500! I have $7500 do I hear $8,000? $8,000? Anyone?" The auctioneer rambled.

"$9500," the mysterious voice called.

"$10,500!" Pearl responded.

"$11." The voice countered.

"$15,000!" Pearl yelled, nearly jumping out of her seat.

"Fifteen?!" Norm yelped, pulling out his wallet to double-check how much cash he brought with him.

"$15,000. Do I hear $15,500? Anyone? $15,500?" The auctioneer called.

Silence filled the auction house.

"We have $15,000. Going, once. Going twice. $15,000 sold to number 63. Please be sure to collect your purchases to the left after the auction closes." The auctioneer instructed as he wrote a large 63 on a yellow sticker and adhered it directly to the front of the safe.

"Yes! We did it!" Pearl yelled, bouncing up and down in her seat with excitement.

"Yes, we certainly did," Norm responded with a worried look on his face. "Let's go collect the thing. You spent every cent we brought."

Pearl smiled broadly as they both stood and began to make their way through the crowd to pick up their merchandise.

The transaction went quickly after Pearl, and Norm reached the cashier's desk. They paid the entirety of their bid plus the percentage toward the auction house and a bidder's fee. When all was said and done, Norm was guiding two young men through the parking lot with $17,250 less than he had before.

"I hope this fits in the truck," Norm mumbled under his breath as they meandered out to the parking space.

"It'll fit, Norm. I know it will." Peal reiterated with enthusiasm.

"We'll have to make it fit, I guess," Norm observed. "Here we are, boys. I don't know how exactly you're going to get it up there, but this is us."

The two young men looked at one another; then looked at Norm and Pearl.

"Sir, this safe weighs a ton, probably two if you want to get technical. How on earth are we supposed to get it inside your truck bed?" One of the young men asked bewildered.

"That's your department." Norm huffed. "An engine dolly might do the trick if you have one around somewhere."

The young men looked at one another and then back at Norm with the same terrified blank expression.

"You don't know what an engine dolly is? It's like a crane. It hoists the engine off of the chassis?" Norm tried to explain.

When the young men didn't change their expression, Norm let out a heavy sigh.

"Okay, I'll call someone to help with it." He relented.

As Norm pulled out his phone, suddenly, the young

men from the auction house lost their grip on the safe. The parking lot wasn't dangerously sloped, but for a several thousand-pound iron box on a dolly, it was enough. The safe began to roll backward and try as they might no one could stop it.

"What on Earth? Hey! Look out!" Norm called as he helplessly watched the two young men bumbling after the safe barreling through the parking lot toward the sidewalk full of pedestrians.

Thankfully before the safe could hit the curb, the momentum surpassed the balance rating of the dolly, and the entire thing tipped over smashing into the concrete as it skidded to a violent stop.

"Well, thank goodness for that." Norm huffed as he hobble jogged to catch up with his runaway merchandise.

"Wow, I'm sorry, sir. I can't believe that happened. I don't know what went wrong." One of the young men stammered, trying to catch his breath.

"No, no, it's okay. We'll figure it all out. How are we going to get it back on the dolly if you couldn't lift it into the truck bed?" Norm asked, bending at the waist and holding his knees, trying to catch his breath.

As soon as he bent over, he noticed a small envelope securely adhered to the bottom of the safe. He took several deep breaths before slowly reaching over and retrieving the envelope.

"What's this?" He asked, standing back to his formidable full height.

He slowly opened the envelope to find a small plastic card with instructions on how to open the safe, complete with the factory assigned combination.

"Wait for a second, wait a second. Before you kill yourself trying to lift that let me see it." Norm instructed, shooing the two young men away from the safe.

He pulled his glasses out of his breast pocket and carefully peered at the display on the safe. It was electronic, but according to the card should have a battery back up system. Norm didn't know how long the battery was supposed to last, or how long the safe had been without power before it made it to the auction house, but he figured that he would give it a try. He tapped the display as instructed, and much to his surprise, it issued a bright blue LED glow and beeped, indicating that it was ready to accept the code.

Norm adjusted his glasses once again, and carefully entered the numbers printed on the card. The safe beeped in protest momentarily; then, as if by magic, the lock tumbled, and the door was ready to open. Norm quickly turned the handle and used all of his remaining strength to open the door upwards.

"What did you find, Norm?" Pearl asked, finally reaching the scene dragging her cane across the ground.

"Jackpot is what I found! Look at this, Pearl! Your intuition was right again!" Norm laughed, pulling out tray after tray of jewelry. "It looks like this safe was where they kept the inventory after hours. I can't even begin to appraise the value of some of these things right now. This safe is amazing, Pearl!"

"Hot damn, I told you so!" Pearl yelled excitedly.

"Well… how about we make you a deal, young man? How about you put all of these trays on that cart and take them back to our truck. You can keep this hunk of junk." Norm asked with a broad smile.

The young men ran inside to consult the situation with their boss. Once things were sorted out with removing the safe from the middle of the parking lot, Norm and Pearl made their way home with a truck cab full of loot. Peal opened each case and inspected the quality of each piece. They were all reasonably standard jeweler quality pieces. Nothing appeared very extravagant, but they would undoubtedly replenish the investment of purchasing the safe in the first place and give their new booth some pizzazz. She almost finished sorting everything when she came upon a small silver bracelet that had fallen from its place in the case and slipped in between the cracks of the velvet lining. She carefully pulled it out and held it up to the light.

It glowed with an internal glow and sparkled in the sun with a radiance she hadn't seen in any of the other pieces.

"Norm, look at this." Peal gasped.

"I can't, dear. I'm driving." Norm answered as he pulled up to an intersection, flipped on his turn signal, and carefully watched oncoming traffic.

"Okay, well, when we stop. This bracelet is magical. It's completely different than the others." Pearl observed as she fastened the bracelet to her wrist.

"I'm sure it is, honey," Norm replied.

Pearl had a habit of embellishing her feelings. She didn't intentionally exaggerate. She got lost in the emotions that consumed her. Norm usually described her as vibrant when speaking to anyone else. He loved her enthusiasm, but he also learned not to get caught up in it. Her intensity would wane soon enough.

Soon they pulled into the parking lot at Ralf's Antiques and Oddities, where they had spent most of their time over the past few months. Pearl wasn't sure why Norm took an interest in antiques as he grew closer to retirement, but she was happy to support him. She spent weeks touring every other booth in the mall, gaining inspiration and ideas for their own. They would be open for business in just a few days, and she was glowing with excitement.

Norm opened the driver's side door and slowly slid out until his feet connected with the pavement. He slowly walked around to the passenger door and dutifully opened it for Pearl. He extended his hand and helped Pearl down to the sidewalk before they both reached in and gathered as many cases of jewelry as they could handle.

Once inside, they smiled at Kim, who ran the front desk and wandered through the maze of various booths until they found their quiet little space near the back of the store. It was the way things worked at Ralf's. When you first rented a booth, you were stuck at the end of the store until you met an individual sales quota. With every successful sale, you moved up in the ranks until you were able to move toward the front of the store. It was a sales union of sorts. Norm wasn't mainly a fan of the way Ralf's chose to run their business, but the booth rent was affordable, and it was something to get him started. If they did well and he enjoyed it, they would likely move elsewhere.

Norm lifted the small yellow rope that closed off their booth for Pearl to carry her load to the nearby table and followed after she was safely through.

"I don't know where we're going to put all of this inventory. We don't have jewelry displays." Pearl mused as she organized her wares into neat stacks until they could figure out what do to with them.

"Hmm…" Norm mused to himself as he added the few cases he carried in with the pile of Pearl's stacks.

He turned a full circle around in the small booth taking stock of everything that they already had displayed. Most of it was random trinkets or old tools they had discovered lingering throughout the old barn on their property. There were a few craft items they picked up at local auctions, and now this plethora of jewelry. It wasn't genuinely antiquated. Still, they each figured that it would fall under the "oddities" category of their adventure with Ralf's.

"Why don't we find a way to prop up these storage cases? All the pieces fit, and it's easy to browse through them." Norm suggested.

"Hey! We can use this empty bookshelf." Peal suggested with glee as she began to open each case and set them carefully on the previously empty shelf.

"That looks great, Peal." Norm encouraged with a smile

as he stepped over to the shelf and began to help his wife organize the cases.

They spent the better part of an hour getting each piece prominently on display, and when they finally finished, they took a step back and admired their work. The booth looked so much brighter as the various stones, chains, and rings refracted the bright fluorescent lights sending little dancing sprites across the entire booth.

"I love it, Norm. This booth is going to be so exciting when we get everything opened next week!" Pearl squealed with delight as she turned to her husband and wrapped her arms around his neck. "Oh. I almost forgot this beauty here."

Pearl brought her arms down and stepped away from Norm back over to the jewelry display shelf as she removed the bracelet from her arm.

"Did you see this, Norm? Look at it. It glows. It glows much brighter than the rest of this silver. It's a special one." Pearl explained, as she gently set the bracelet into a case to display it.

Norm wandered over and peered at the bracelet. It did seem to issue a shine that was significantly different than the rest of the silverware they received in the lot.

"That's odd." He mused, adjusting his glasses and reaching out to pick up the bracelet.

As soon as his finger made contact with the bracelet, a warmth somewhat like electricity flowed through his hand. He jerked his hand away in surprise.

"What was that?" Pearl laughed.

"It... I don't know. It felt hot?" Norm grumbled, reaching for the bracelet again. "Do you know what this symbol means?"

Pearl hadn't noticed the inscription before. She assumed it was a benign design, but once Norm pointed it out, she couldn't help but take notice.

"I don't know that it means anything, Norm. Remember

that trend a few years back? Everyone wanted something with Chinese or Japanese writing on it. I bet this is just leftover from that phase. It probably means luck or something." Pearl explained.

"Take a picture of it. If I'm going to sell it, I want to know what it means." Norm insisted as he stepped away from the bracelet, gently rubbing his hand that still tingled with the after-effects of electric shock.

"You don't think it's anything special, do you, Norm?" Peal said with a chuckle as she dug through her large quilted handbag in search of her cell phone.

"I don't know. You can't be too careful with things like that, Pearl. You might not believe it, but I've seen things when I was overseas during the war. It's real to some people, and we need to respect that." Norm said factually.

Pearl scoffed as she finally found her cell phone and wandered over to the small shelf to snap a quick picture of the bracelet to appease her superstitious husband. He was right. She didn't believe in the good luck charms of many traditional Asian cultures, but she had never left the United States. She never argued with Norm when he spoke of his several tours of duty overseas during the various conflicts of the late 50s and 60s. It had changed him in significant ways that she would likely never understand.

She hoped that this brief argument wouldn't send Norm into a dark thought spiral and bring up his nightmares again. So many years had passed since he returned from the war and retired from the military that he didn't often encounter the flashbacks and depression as he did in his younger days. Every once in a while, something like this would send him down that dark path once again.

"Norm, honey? Are you okay?" Pearl asked, noticing the grey pallor fall over Norm's usually vibrant disposition as she returned her phone to her handbag.

"What? Oh yes. I'm fine. Just tired from gathering all of these things and setting everything up. I'm ready to head home." Norm answered, still looking quite pale.

"Okay, Norm. That sounds like a good idea. I'll make chicken and dumplings tonight. It seems like a good night for that." Peal encouraged, gently placing her hand on Norm's arm.

Norm flinched and began to pace back and forth the slight sheen of a cold sweat beginning to break across his forehead. It was going to be a difficult night, Pearl could sense the change in her husband, and it brought tears to her eyes.

The next morning, Pearl slipped quietly out of the house before Norm woke up. He had been up most of the night and had finally settled into a deep sleep as daybreak peeked over the horizon. On days when he didn't remember the horrors he endured in war, he was usually up before the sun puttering around the house, working on various projects of one vein or another.

Pearl wasn't sure how early Ralf's would be open to vendors before the store itself opened. It was something she never looked into since Norm was in charge of the technical aspects of their booth. She glanced at her delicate gold wristwatch as she climbed into her small compact car. It was almost 7 am. Surely someone would let her into the building since the store itself was scheduled to open at 8 am. She took a deep breath and started her car.

The small engine sputtered and coughed until it eventually roared to life. They didn't often use Pearl's small car since it was difficult for Norm to fit his ample frame behind the steering wheel. She didn't usually drive these days, preferring to leave the stress of navigating traffic to Norm, but this was important. She needed to sell the bracelet, or at least trade it with another vendor. He would never admit to it, but it deeply affected Norm. Pearl wasn't about to watch her husband suffer any more than he already had.

It took several moments to adjust to driving again, and she was thankful for their long gravel driveway, which provided her with much-needed practice before entering the highway. Once she reached the road, she puttered along just below the speed limit until she reached the shopping plaza where Ralf's was one of the only things remaining.

She chose a spot close to the door and made her way toward the store. She crept up onto the sidewalk and peered into the large plate glass sliding doors. Normally they squeaked reliably and sputtered open as soon as you made your way in front of them. It was foreign to Pearl to walk up to sliding doors without the reassuring squeak and sputter. She felt a little bit uneasy and a lot out of place.

She could see Kim milling around behind the sales counter, but she couldn't think of an appropriate way to get her attention. Pearl tapped on the glass doors, first with her fist, then with her car keys to issue a sharper sound. On her third try, Kim finally looked in Pearl's direction. She hesitated at first, unsure of why Pearl was there before store hours. Eventually, she slowly walked over and unlocked the second set of sliding doors before stepping into the vestibule.

"Pearl? Is that you? What do you want? Is everything okay?" Kim asked, taking a nervous glance around the parking lot to make sure Pearl hadn't been followed or wasn't in distress.

"Hi Kim, yes. I need to rearrange some inventory at the booth. Norm isn't feeling very well today, and I wanted to get it out of the way before we came in to open up this afternoon." Peal answered with a smile.

"We don't usually allow vendors in the building before we open…" Kim began.

"Oh, oh, I know. It's just that I must do this for Norm." Pearl repeated, hoping that her insistence would convey her urgency.

Kim hesitated and took another thorough glance around

the parking lot before finally flipping the latch to the last remaining set of sliding doors and allowing Pearl inside the shop.

"Hurry up. It's dangerous to unlock the doors before we open, and Ben gets here." Kim insisted, ushering Pearl into the vestibule before quickly locking the doors behind her. "I hate when they have me open by myself, but sometimes it just can't be helped."

"Thank you. I appreciate it. Norm will too." Pearl said as she wobbled through the vestibule and headed directly toward her booth.

"Please be careful back there. I won't be able to hear or help you if something falls." Kim pleaded before returning to her duties behind the sales counter.

Pearl nodded and made her way through the maze of booths back to her own. Everything was as she'd left it the night before, which was a relief after bringing in so many high priced items. She crawled underneath the yellow rope stretched across the opening of the booth and puttered her way around to the bookshelf baring the jewelry. She opened one case and then another. Soon, she realized that she couldn't remember where she put the bracelet.

"Oh, come on." She huffed in frustration. "Now, where are you?"

She opened several more cases and still couldn't find the bracelet. The more cases she opened and turned up empty-handed, the more her frustration began to turn to panic. Soon she was opening cases and haphazardly tossing them to the floor, recklessly spilling the contents everywhere. Soon she had opened every case and still couldn't find the bracelet. She collapsed onto the floor and began to weep as she looked at her watch. She spent an hour looking through everything, and Norm would be waking up soon. She had failed in her mission, and now she had a mess to clean up too.

"Are you okay?" A voice called, bringing Pearl out of

her self-loathing stupor.

She looked up to see a girl, probably no more than 21, peering over the yellow rope with concern riddled across her face.

"Oh, yes, honey. I'm fine. Just a little discouraged is all. I was looking for something special, and I fear that I've lost it." Pearl explained, wiping the tears from her eyes.

"Can I help you at all?" The girl asked, sincerely.

Pearl smiled.

"You sure can. I need some help cleaning up this mess. My old bones don't cooperate like they used to." Pearl explained.

"Hold on. Let me tell my friends where I went. I'll be right back." The girl explained as she rushed down the aisleway.

She quickly returned, ducked under the yellow rope, and gently helped Pearl to her feet.

"Thank you, honey," Pearl said, taking a seat in the one folding chair that she and Norm kept at the booth. "If you could just set those cases on this table here, I'll get the jewelry put back together."

"Okay. I'm Nina, by the way. Nice to meet you, Ms…" Nina said, extending her hand.

"Pearl. You can call me Pearl." Pearl answered, taking Nina's small hand and offering a firm handshake.

Nina smiled as she began to gingerly pick up the cases and jewelry strewn across the floor of the small booth.

"What brings you to Ralf's so early on a Wednesday, Nina?" Peal asked as she began to untangle a silver chain and wrap it carefully around the velvet-lined peg in the display case.

"I run an online boutique. It helps me pay for my books and other college expenses. It's not a lot, but it's something. I like to come here and pick up the inventory. Wednesdays are the days that most vendors add new stock." Nina explained, crawling under a shelf to retrieve the last few items and deliver them to the table for Pearl.

"That's wonderful, dear. What are you studying?" Pearl asked.

"Elementary education. I want to be a teacher." Nina answered, reaching her arm as far back toward the wall as she could. There was something stuck around the back leg of the shelf.

"That's an extraordinary calling. It's good to see young people invested in their futures as well as the futures of others. It's not something you see very often these days. Not to sound ageist or perpetuate the generation divide. I'm just an old lady speaking from experience." Pearl explained. "Are you alright, dear?"

"Yes. There is something stuck back here. I'm just trying to reach it." Nina explained straining to untangle the object from the leg of the shelf.

Finally, the object came loose, and she was able to retrieve it.

"Wow." She gasped as she pulled the bracelet out from under the shelf ad held it up to the light.

"Nina! You've found it!" Pearl yelped with excitement.

"It's beautiful. How much do you want for it? I'd love to have it for my boutique." Nina asked as she stood, completely mesmerized by the bracelet.

"You can have it, dear. Think of it as payment for all of your help this morning. I want you to take it." Pearl said, taking Nina's hands and wrapping them around the bracelet.

"Oh, I couldn't possibly..." Nina began to argue.

"No, no. This is an extraordinary piece. It was meant to be a gift. It never needed to be sold. That's why I was looking for it. You deserve it. I insist. Now please, take it before I chase you out of my booth with this cane." Pearl insisted with a smile and a wink as she shook her cane in Nina's direction.

Nina smiled.

"Thank you, Ms. Pearl."

9 FATE

Nina tucked the bracelet safely into her pocket, bid Pearl goodbye, and quickly hurried down the aisles in search of her friends. Once she found them, they continued to browse the rest of the booths throughout Ralf's until they each had a pile of trinkets and eclectic collectibles. They made their way to the purchase counter, where Kim quickly rang them up, and then they headed back to the state university dorms where they all lived. Nina rarely left the campus without her roommate Sydnee. She didn't like the hustle and bustle of big city life.

As her name implied, Nina had grown up on a rural farm. She was the first person in three generations to pursue higher education. Not only had she taken the initiative to go to college, but she also chose the state university because it was in the state capital. She longed for adventure and something different aside from the small convenience store, local library, and movie theater where she spent most of her youth. The town where she was born was so small that it didn't even have a bowling alley. It was the classic definition of the one-stoplight town, and while she could appreciate small-town life for what it was, she longed for something more.

Something more is what she received when she began attending the university. Then she realized how terrifying big city life could be. The one time she left campus alone, she was followed and accosted by a group of men. Thankfully, she was able to duck into a gas station where the attendant gave her shelter. She still shuddered to think about what might have happened if she hadn't been so lucky.

Sydnee was driving, and soon pulled into the large parking structure reserved for students at the university. She expertly navigated the small lanes of the structure until she found her assigned space, and quickly pulled in.

"Same time next week?" Nina cheerfully asked the other passengers in the back seat.

"Sure. Sounds great. We'll text you." They both replied as they exited the car and headed toward the elevator.

"Do you think they're going to text me, Sed?" Nina asked as she watched the two board the elevator.

"I don't know, Daze. Who wants to hang out with them anyway? They were boring and didn't appreciate the great feather boa I found." Sydnee answered with a reassuring smile.

"That's true. That boa is pretty amazing." Nina said, pulling the boa out of Sydnee's shopping bag and throwing it around her neck. "It's marvelous, darling." She quipped emulating an exaggerated fashionista persona.

Her facade soon crumbled as she and Sydnee filled the small sedan with laugher.

"Let's get inside. It's cold out here today." Sydnee encouraged, reaching into the back seat and gathering her shopping bags and a few other belongings.

"It is a little bit chilly." Nina agreed. She issued a shiver as she gathered her belongings and followed Sydnee out of the car and quickly across the parking structure to the skyway connecting it to their dorm.

They briskly walked across the skyway and through the crowded and loud hallways of the dorm until they reached the quiet and safety of their room. Sydnee unlocked the door, and both girls spilled through it as quickly as possible before collapsing onto their beds.

"Whew. I think it gets crazier and crazier every time we leave this place." Nina mused.

"Maybe. Or maybe we pick the worst times to get out because we have the most unusual class schedules?" Sydnee observed.

"Maybe." Nina agreed, closing her eyes and relishing the quiet of their dorm while the rest of their classmates and fellow students milled around outside.

"Speaking of class schedules, I think I'm about to be late for poly-sci. I better grab my notes and go. I'll see you this evening for dinner, okay?" Sydnee said as she stood up and quickly grabbed her backpack before rushing out the door.

"Okay," Nina called after her.

Once she had the room to herself, Nina began to unpack the bags from Ralf's and take photographs of each item she planned on adding to her inventory. She didn't have any classes scheduled for today, and she enjoyed filling her time with the boutique. It kept her mind off her anxiety and gave her something productive to do in her small home.

She added an embroidered lampshade, a pair of purple velvet slacks, fedora with a large red feather, two silver candlesticks. Then she reached into her pocket and pulled out the bracelet. When Pearl first gave it to her, she had intended to keep it, but now she wasn't so sure. It felt powerful but in a dangerous way. As if it belonged to someone else, and only the intended owner could correctly wield its power. As that thought crossed her mind, Nina had to smile. Did she really believe that nonsense? She didn't know, but she didn't particularly care to keep it around and find out.

She arranged the chain around the pendant on a carefully selected background to highlight it's size, shape, and brilliance. She pulled out her phone, adjusted the camera settings to something that she liked, then snapped several pictures. When she finished, she placed the bracelet in a small organizer drawer and set about uploading the images of her new inventory to her online boutique.

Life had taken Jen and Connor along some unexpected paths. They married soon after Jen moved in, and their relationship had been excellent, yet deeply complicated. No matter how hard she tried, Jen couldn't seem to move past Nate and the feelings she felt toward him. Of course, it didn't help that Nate would frequently contact her and play with her mind and heart. Even when the emails, phone calls, and social media messages from Nate began to fade, she still struggled with the ugliness that happened between them.

Connor was wonderfully supportive in the beginning. While his support for his wife never wavered, the rest of their relationship became strained. Things only became worse when Jen gave birth to their first child, then two more quickly after the first. Having three small children to tend to, on top of the already strained relationship, proved almost impossible.

Jen did everything in her power to keep her marriage afloat, and tend to her children. Finally, she took the necessary steps to address her mental health as well as her physical health. She found herself in intensive therapy and discovered that she had Post Traumatic Stress Disorder. Once she could put a name to the reason her relationship with Nate continued to haunt her, an entirely new world of tools and techniques opened to her. Slowly, things began to improve. Her moods began to stabilize, and she was no longer thrown under a proverbial bus if Nate chose to reach out to her.

As Jen came to terms with the severity of Nate's mistreatment during their relationship, she soon realized the significance of Charli's precious gifts to her. Charli wasn't just polite. Charli recognized her son's abusive behavior toward Jen immediately and subtly expressed her displeasure and alliance with the sentimental and powerful Kanji gift. As soon as the puzzle pieces of Charli's true intentions clicked together in Jen's fractured mind, she felt awful for giving it away.

At first, Jen assumed she could find another to match her original. She believed the lies that Nate told her about his mother's flippant disregard for others. Soon, however, Jen realized that the gifts were even more precious than a sentimental silent message. She couldn't find a replica anywhere. She looked high and low. Online and offline. She scoured department store shelves, jeweler's catalogs, and even online auction sites. She could visualize the Kanji inscribed, and she knew the meaning, but still, she couldn't find anything to match the necklace Charli had given her.

Months turned into years, and still, Jen's search proved fruitless. Just as she was about to give up altogether and begin looking for anything else that she could bestow the significance on, suddenly, a bracelet populated in her search results. It seemed vaguely familiar, but nothing like her original necklace. She studied the pictures and looked at the price. It wasn't a terrible price for what the seller was offering, and maybe she could alter the chain or make the pendant into a slide for a necklace. Her hand hovered over the purchase button as her thoughts raced around, and she attempted to calm herself to make a rational decision.

Finally, after several hours with the bracelet in her cart, she took the plunge and hit the purchase button. She took a deep breath and sent a silent wish into the universe. If it were meant to be hers, it would find her.

Nina was startled when the notification sounded, and

her phone buzzed in her hand. She was in the middle of a challenging level of an online game. All of her concentration invested in it. Since the game automatically paused when the notification rang through, she decided to click on the banner. She sold something from her boutique, and she was curious exactly which item had sold. To her surprise, it was the small silver Kanji bracelet she listed just days earlier. The one thing that she was sure no one would buy flew off of her cyber shelf.

"Wow. That's so weird. I'll have to remember to get it in the mail this week." Nina mumbled to herself, closing the notification window and returning to her game.

Several days passed, and still, the bracelet had yet to be marked as shipped. Jen was beginning to suspect that the listing was either a fake or forgotten. She returned to the website and pulled up her sales receipt, which included the purchase listing and clicked through to see how old the listing was and the location where she could expect it to ship.

As she read through the listing, she discovered that it had only been online for a few days before she purchased it. The seller had a high rating and a quick shipping reputation. It was odd that she had yet to ship the item, and then Jen read the city of origin.

"What? No way. No way!" Jen yelped from in front of her computer, startling her two youngest children who had been quietly watching TV.

"What's wrong, mommy?" One of her children asked as they peeked over the back of the couch and peered in Jen's direction.

"Oh, nothing, baby. I was just a little bit surprised, that's all. Everything is okay. Watch your movie." Jen answered, trying not to choke or have her eyes well up with tears.

The city of shipping origin was the city Jen had left behind at the end of her relationship with Nate. She clicked the listing again and stared at the bracelet. Could it be? She was awestruck, overwhelmed, excited, and apprehensive, all at once. She wanted to know where the seller found it, but this particular boutique didn't offer any private communication. Jen felt silly asking such a personal question, as in where did the seller acquire the item, but she had to know.

After several hours of debate, and what seemed like a hundred different drafts of a quick comment, Jen finally submitted her question:

"Hi there. This is kind of weird, but I just noticed where you were shipping from. I was wondering where you first got this item, do you remember?"

Jen held her breath as she waited for a reply. She had no idea what the seller might be doing or when or even if she would respond. Jen's hand shook as she held her phone, waiting for a notification to come through. When nothing arrived after several moments, she put her phone away. She began to clean her house nervously and tend to her children, desperately trying to keep her mind occupied and grounded.

After several hours of silence, finally, Jen's phone issued the cheerful chirp of a notification from the boutique. She dropped the dishes she was washing, quickly dried her hands, and raced to her phone where she read the carefully penned response from the seller:

"Hi, I'm sorry. I don't remember. I believe I got it at an auction or maybe a local antique mall. I'll get it in the mail for you tomorrow."

The response was vague, and not at all what Jen had hoped to receive. Jen was left with the same mystery that she began with. It was encouraging, however, to hear that the seller would be shipping the item out the next day. At least the listing wasn't fake, even if the bracelet ended up being something entirely different from what Jen was expecting.

Jen kept herself busy the rest of the day tidying up the house and tending to her kids. Soon Connor arrived home from work, and she excitedly shared the news with him.

"So... remember how I told you Charli, Nate's mom, gave me that necklace for Christmas one year?" Jen asked as Connor walked in the front door to an excited chorus of 'Daddy!!' and other illegible squeals from the kids.

"Yeah, I think so. What about it?" Connor answered, scooping up the two youngest kids and giving them a giant hug while the oldest danced around his legs.

"I was browsing around online today, and I think I found it. Well, no, not IT, but a part of the set. It was fairly affordable, so I bought it, right? Then I looked at the city of origin and... it's from home Connor." Jen explained, trying to hold back the tears that began to sting her eyes and calm her children as they continued to jump up and down.

Connor looked at Jen's conflicted emotional face and processed what she had just told him. Unannounced to her, Connor had been searching for the jewelry as well. He had come up just as empty-handed as Jen. Now, to find a piece in the same city where Jen received her original piece was extraordinary as well as exciting.

"Wow. That's crazy." Connor answered, setting the kids down and finally wrapping his arms around his wife. "I'm glad you found it."

"The seller is going to ship it tomorrow. I won't know if it's part of my original set until it arrives, but yeah. It's been a day." Jen squeaked as she sank into Connor's arms.

Nina's alarm went off much earlier than she was expecting. She groaned and rolled over to hit the snooze button, but before she could find it, Sydnee flipped on her bedside lamp.

"Wake up, sleepyhead! You promised to ship those items to your customers before class this morning. You have half an hour." Sydnee called as she pulled the alarm clock off of Nina's desk and grabbed the corner of her blanket, wrenching it from her friend who had curled up in a vain attempt to stop her.

"Customers... ugh." Nina groaned as the cool bedroom air hit her skin, causing her to curl into an even tighter ball attempting to retain her warmth.

"Girl, you know you need to get up and do this. You've been putting it off all week. Why?" Sydnee asked playfully, poking at Nina's ribs.

"I don't know. Quit it." Nina answered, giving up her fight to remain warm and sleepy and sitting up in her bed, batting Sydnee's hand away.

"Seriously, Daze. You're usually on top of it, but you're slacking with these orders. What's wrong?" Sydnee prodded.

"It's not all of the orders. I've shipped most of them. It's just this last one." Nina answered, reaching over to her small desk organizer and pulling the bracelet out.

"Wow. Where did you get that? I don't remember you buying it at Ralf's." Sydnee gasped as she admired the bracelet from across the room.

"I did get it from Ralf's, but I didn't buy it. That's the thing. It was a gift from this older lady who I helped clean up some spilled inventory. She gave it to me as payment. She said it was special, and it didn't need to be merchandise, but given away. What did I do? I turned around and sold it, and now I'm having second thoughts." Nina explained as she held the bracelet in her palm and watched the light reflect off of it and bounce around the room.

"So, explain that to the buyer. Or just tell them you lost it or something and give them a refund. You don't have to sell it. One negative rating won't make or break the boutique." Sydnee suggested.

"I thought about that, but then the buyer commented on the listing. She's excited about it. I'd feel awful about disappointing her now. I promised I would ship it out today. That's why I set the alarm. I... I don't know if I'm doing the right thing, Sed." Nina mused as she glanced at the clock hanging from their wall.

"Well," Sydnee said as she followed Nina's gaze to the clock, "you have about fifteen minutes to figure it out."

"Yeah…" Nina mumbled as she continued to watch the reflections from the bracelet dance around the room.

Both girls sat in silence for several moments as the reflections glittered back and forth as the angle of the light from the bedside table and the rising sun competed against the silver surface.

"Okay. I'm going to ship it. I have to. It's too late to turn back now." Nina exclaimed as she jumped up from her bed, quickly changed into sweat pants and a hooded sweatshirt, and dashed out the door.

She hurried through the corridor of the dorm building until she reached the annex that led toward the library. She quickly turned and made her way into the library, which also served as the local campus post office. The bracelet was snuggled safely into her kangaroo pocket. She reached the small post counter and selected the smallest bubble mailer that she could find.

Usually, she would send a cute note or wrap her wares in a bright package. Today, she wanted to get the box out of her hands and on its way before she changed her mind. She printed the postage at the postage kiosk, then made her way to the postage counter, dropped the small package with the attendant, turned, and walked away.

It was over with now. Nina could only hope that she made the right decision.

10 HOMECOMING

The package sat on the postage counter unnoticed until late afternoon as the attendant began to close the stand. Nina left in such a hurry, and the packaging was so small that he didn't noticed it until he began closing the security gate. He quietly tossed the box into the collection bin, where it went through the process of weights and measures. Then it was loaded onto a semi-trailer where it spent several days jostling around as it traveled hundreds of miles. Eventually, the truck came to a stop at another small post office, and the package was unloaded and tossed onto a conveyer belt for sorting.

The package was again scanned and sent to the correct chute, and lined up with many other packages and letters scheduled for delivery. It sat in the chute for several hours as each other package and letter was carefully sorted and bundled before being loaded into a postal truck. Soon it was lifted from the chute and tossed haphazardly into the back of a postal truck. The door was closed, and off it went bumbling along in the trailer until it reached its final destination: Jen McAlister.

Jen was sitting outside watching her children play in the

back yard, keeping herself occupied with a warm cup of coffee and trivial game on her phone. She had impatiently been waiting for the mail to arrive all afternoon. The driver on the route through Jen's neighborhood was less than reliable. They made a delivery each day, but the time was never consistent.

Finally, she heard the familiar diesel rumble of the delivery truck as it made its way through the neighborhood. She had to stop herself from running out to wait by the mailbox like a child. Instead, she stood from her chair, stretched her legs, and casually sauntered toward the front of the house.

"I'll be right back, guys. I'm just running up to the front to check the mail." Jen called to her children as they continued to swing and play happily in the sand.

She opened the back door and jogged through the house. She watched the delivery driver open her mailbox, insert several items, and continue toward her neighbor's house. She gasped when she didn't see a package inside the mailbox. She carefully removed each piece of mail and sorted through it. Still, she didn't find anything even remotely resembling a box. She was frustrated as she looked through the letters once again, hoping that she missed it.

"Excuse me! Ma'am? I'm sorry. I just saw this." The delivery driver called as he jogged from his truck back toward Jen.

"Ah-ha! I was looking for that. Thank you!" Jen yelped in relief as she also jogged over to meet the driver and receive the small package in his hand.

"No problem. Have a good day." The driver huffed, attempting to catch his breath as he turned and walked back toward his truck.

"Thank you, you too!" Jen called after him as she excitedly ripped open the packaging.

As soon as she spilled the bracelet into her hand, a feeling of warmth and recognition came over her. A broad smile spread across her face as she pulled the charm closer to her face to give it a more thorough inspection. As she examined the lines and wear marks etched into the pendant after years of love and neglect, she knew: it was her pendant.

"I bet you have a hundred stories to tell, don't you little guy?" Jen whispered as she quickly fastened the bracelet to her wrist and made her way back to her kids playing in the back yard.

She watched the bracelet twist and turn, reflecting the late summer sunlight with its iridescent internal glow. A warm breeze gently blew past her, sending the pendant spinning once again as emotion began to overwhelm her.

"Thank you, Charli. Thank you." Jen whispered to herself as a single tear dripped down each of her cheeks.

She quietly wiped the tears from her eyes and glanced at the pendant one more time before sitting down on the edge of the sandbox and embracing the happiness, which now surrounded her inside and out.

Jen continued to watch her children play until the sun reached its afternoon peak. She then ushered everyone inside. She quickly made peanut butter and jelly sandwiches for lunch, and after everyone ate their fill, she quietly tucked each of her little ones into their beds for nap time. Once she was sure each of her children was sleeping soundly, Jen sat down at her computer desk. She began to work on several spreadsheets that had been patiently waiting in her inbox.

Soon after she and Connor were married, Jen had the opportunity to cut her hours and work from home. She enjoyed the freedom and comfort of making her schedule. It significantly helped as she began to detox from the abuse she endured with Nate as well. Sometimes she missed interacting with her coworkers face to face. Still, in the end, she was grateful to remain employed while also being present for her children.

Her youngest had enrolled in the local kindergarten for the upcoming school year. Soon she would have no excuses to stay sequestered inside of her home. She was conflicted. On the one hand, she was thrilled with the prospect of returning to the workforce. On the other, she was apprehensive about returning to a rigid work schedule, office politics, and the long commute to and from the office each day.

Jen paused in her work, adjusted her glasses, and took a long sip from her lukewarm coffee as she stared at her computer monitor. All she had to do for this client was some simple online banner ads. It should have been a quick and easy process. Yet, this particular customer was quite adamant about how he wanted his ads to appear. Jen had been trying to avoid it for months, but now it seemed that a trip to speak with the customer face to face was in order.

She reached for her phone and dialed the contact number included on the signature line of her correspondence emails. The phone buzzed as the line connected. She waited patiently until a cheerful voice answered on the other end of the line.

"Hello. Yes. This is Jen McAlister of Jinks Marketing? Yes, I've been working closely with Mr. Johnson regarding the new advertising campaign. I was wondering if it would be possible to set up a meeting next week? Email and phone conferences aren't quite working to convey my intent. I'd rather meet with him face to face if possible." Jen explained. "Yes. Friday afternoon? I can make it work. Thank you so much. I look forward to meeting him. Yes. Thank you."

Jen ended the call and sat leaned back into her chair. Then she picked up the phone one more time and dialed her boss. She needed to make travel arrangements to New York.

"Hey, Jackie, it's Jen. I need to book a flight and a two-night stay in New York. This client is driving a hard sell. I can't communicate effectively on the phone or through email. I set up a meeting with his secretary. I just need to get there. Next Friday. Yep. No, I don't care about first-class or five stars. Thanks. You're the best. Check your email for the rest of my spreadsheets. I sent them over this morning. Sounds good." Jen said as she ended the call and closed her computer.

Her children were beginning to stir from their naps, and it was time to get dinner preparations in order. Work would have to wait.

The sound of the telephone ring echoed off the hotel room wall, stirring Jen from sleep. She never slept well away from home and had been working late into the night. She opened her eyes to find that she fell asleep in the middle of preparing a presentation for Mr. Johnson. Several additional slides had appeared, and things had rearranged before she fell into a deep sleep.

"Great." She mumbled as she sat up, closed her computer, and answered the shrill telephone. "Hello, Jen McAlister."

"Good morning, Ms. McAlister. This is your wake up call at 9 am. Have a good day." An electronic voice called out from the other end of the line.

Jen grumbled incoherently and returned the receiver to the cradle. She rolled out of bed and stumbled into the small bathroom.

"Good Lord, I look like I've been hit by a truck." She exclaimed as she examined her reflection. She had fallen asleep in the same clothes she arrived in the day before, and her makeup smudged beyond recognition. She needed a shower, pressed pantsuit, and large coffee as soon as possible.

She left her disheveled appearance in the mirror and turned to the shower. She adjusted the water temperature to her liking, quickly shed her clothes, and stepped into the refreshing warm water. The grime of travel and discomforts of hotel life washed away as Jen rinsed her thick hair before pausing to enjoy the warm water splashing quietly against her skin.

She soon turned off the water and stepped out onto the cold bathroom tiles, where she quickly dried and dressed in her favorite pinstripe suit. It always inspired a level of confidence that she didn't feel without it. In a way, it was her good luck charm. Mr. Johnson seemed kind enough in her previous interactions with him. However, Jen was so out of practice in one on one sales that he was exceptionally nervous about meeting with him.

She finished pulling on her pants and buttoning her blouse, threw her hair into a smart yet simple top knot, brushed on eyeshadow, some mascara, and finally a pastel peach lipstick.

"Well, that's as good as it's going to get. Time to go meet this Jack Johnson fellow." Jen mused as she slipped on her wedding ring, a simple set of earrings, and finished her look by adding the bracelet.

After it returned to her, Jen rarely took the bracelet off. She shared her excitement and wonder with Connor, and he was thrilled as well as dumbfounded that the very pendant Jen lost found its way back to her. It was nothing short of a miracle. She cherished the bracelet and the feelings of warmth and comfort it brought each time she wore it.

She smiled as she admired the small Kanji charm spinning back and forth as it delicately hung from her wrist.

"Well, Little Charm, it's time to strut your stuff. Finalizing this deal will bring me some happiness." Jen chuckled as she stepped into her shoes and packed up her laptop before heading out to fetch a cab downtown to Mr. Johnson's office.

While she had never spent much time in a large city like New York, Jen was able to blend in fairly well on the city streets. She stepped out of the large hotel lobby onto the sidewalk. She quickly made her way to the curb, where she was fortunate enough to snag a taxi immediately.

"Johnson Tower, please," Jen instructed the driver.
He nodded, set the meter, and pulled out into traffic.

Jen stared out the window at the passing scenery. It was almost like driving through the set of a movie as they passed by the park, through each eclectic neighborhood, and eventually came to a stop at an impressive highrise. Jen paid her cab fare and stepped out onto the busy sidewalk. She didn't frequently contend with sidewalk traffic in addition to auto traffic. It took her a moment to gain her bearings before she moved forward to the large rotating doors and shuffled her way into the expansive lobby.

"Wow," She gasped, pausing out of the pedestrian traffic flow to take in the intricate office design and company logos prominently displayed throughout the room. "How did Jackie land a client like this?"

"Hey, can I help you? Are you lost?" A formidable security guard yelled from behind a large desk just in front of the elevator bank.

Hearing his rough voice snapped Jen out of a stupor, and she quickly approached the desk.

"Yes, I'm sorry. I'm looking for Mr. Johnson's office. I have a meeting at noon. Jen McAlister with Jinks Marketing." Jen explained as she fumbled with her messenger bag in search of her company ID.

"Take that elevator to the top floor. You can check in with Becky when you get there." The security guard explained, brushing Jen's ID out of his reach as he gestured to the elevator bank.

"Oh… okay. Thank you." Jen answered with an involuntary scowl as she put her ID back into her bag and headed toward the elevator.

She pressed the arrow, indicating the direction she wished to travel and took a few steps back patiently, waiting for the doors to open. Before long, the doors slid open, and she stepped inside. She expected the carriage to be crowded and full. Much to her surprise, the doors slid quietly closed with no other passengers boarding. She glanced around the cab and spotted a single button on the side panel next to the emergency phone. She pressed the button, and the carriage shot upward with surprising speed, nearly knocking her off balance.

Before she realized what was happening, the elevator carriage slowed to a stop, and the doors once again flew open. Jen could feel the building beneath her feer rocking and swaying in the wind as she stepped from the elevator carriage into the small lobby. As she entered the lobby, she found a single large desk and several chairs arranged in sort of a waiting room area. There was a modern accent table with several stacks of different publications, a few house plants, and even a small television displaying the local news.

Jen began to walk toward the desk as she continued to survey the room and search for the receptionist she assumed remained posted at the counter.

"I guess it is fairly close to lunchtime," Jen spoke to herself, taking a seat in the chair closest to the desk. She pulled out her phone and glanced at the time. It was 11:45 am — the meeting scheduled for noon.

She decided to give the office a call in hopes that the receptionist had forwarded her phone to someone else within the office itself. She dialed the number and held her phone to her ear. Much to her disappointment, the phone at the abandoned reception desk began to ring. She waited to see if the phone would forward after a certain number of rings. When it clicked over to voicemail instead, she ended the call. As she sat her phone down in her lap, she glanced at the time once again. It was now 11:50 am, and still, there was no one to let her into the office or even alert Mr. Johnson that she had arrived.

"Ms. McAlister?" A polite masculine voice called from behind her.

Jen jumped and turned to find the source of the voice. When she did, she found a kind looking older gentleman in a well-tailored suit.

"Yes. Mr. Johnson, I presume?" Jen asked, standing and extending her hand outward in a handshake.

"Yes, hello. I'm sorry to leave you waiting out here. Becky is normally quite prompt about forwarding her phone. Please step into my office, and we can get started." Jack answered, taking Jen's hand and returning her shake.

Jack stepped to the side and opened a hidden doorway that led directly into his office. He ushered Jen inside and followed behind her.

"Your building is beautiful, Mr. Johnson. Who designed it?" Jen asked setting her bag on a large marble conference table

"Thank you, I did. Before I took over the company for my father, I was an architect by trade. This building was my gift to him before he passed." Jack explained. "Unfortunately, it was one of the only things I was able to design before I was required to take over the company."

"I'm sorry, Mr. Johnson. I think I understand what your vision for the advertisement campaign is now. If I had known you were an artist yourself..." Jen began as she rolled up her blouse sleeves in preparation to deliver her presentation.

"Where did you get that?" Jack rudely interrupted. It was out of character for him to be so blunt, but the moment Jen rolled up her sleeve, he spotted the Kanji on her bracelet, and his heart lept into his throat.

"I'm sorry, what?" Jen asked as her train of thought was swiftly derailed by Mr. Johnson's unusual question.

"That bracelet. Where did you get it?" Jack clarified.

"Oh, well, that's quite a story actually," Jen answered absentmindedly bringing the bracelet closer to her chest. "Several years ago, I received it as a gift. Originally it was a necklace. I lost it for a while, but I just recently found it online of all places. Somewhere during our time apart, it's been pretty beaten up and eventually made into this bracelet. It's very precious to me. It means…"

"Happiness. Yes, I'm aware. You said it was a necklace when you received it the first time. Do you know where it came from? May I look at it?" Jack asked, once again forgetting his manners and interrupting Jen.

Jen hesitated, still holding the bracelet close to her heart. She had no idea what about the bracelet had seemed so important to Mr. Johnson. Yet, his swift change in character and intensity began to make her feel uneasy.

"I'm sorry, Ms. McAlister. I didn't mean to frighten you. Here, let me show you something. You don't have to show me the bracelet if it makes you uncomfortable." Jack reassured, noticing that Jen's body language had quickly gone from a confident businesswoman to a timid and insecure shell.

Jack turned on a projector hanging from the ceiling and connected it to his phone, where he opened up his photo library and scrolled through many photos of his family. She watched his two children go from school-age kids to infants. Eventually, the images only included himself and his wife. First through her late pregnancy, and then beyond.

Jen was even more uncomfortable now than she had been when Mr. Johnson began asking about her bracelet. It was highly unusual to be privileged to someone's private life in this way, especially when she had only just met him.

"Ah, here we go. I believe you were given the same necklace that I commissioned for my wife nearly eleven years ago, Ms. McAlister. We lost our first pregnancy on the eve of her cancer diagnosis. She barely survived the treatments combined with the grief. I almost lost her." Jack explained. "The day I gave her this necklace, she went into a miraculous remission. Soon after, we were blessed with our twins. She lost the necklace holiday shopping several years ago. I never thought we would see it again. Let alone, like this. If it's not the same piece, the resemblance is remarkable." Jack said, settling on a photo of his wife wearing a necklace bearing the same iridescent shine and Kanji as the bracelet around Jen's wrist.

Jen gasped as she stepped closer to the wall reflecting the photo from the projection.

"Mr. Johnson, that's incredible. I'm so sorry for your loss."

"Thank you; it was a challenging time for Tabitha. Has the Kanji served you well?" Jack asked. "Has it brought you happiness?"

"Yes. Great happiness: my husband and my children. It brought me peace from the torment of my past. It brought me the courage to continue moving forward with my new life and the strength to hold my abusive ex-boyfriend accountable for his crimes. I would say it served me well." Jen answered.

"This might be a bit out of line for me to ask, but do you suppose we could visit the silversmith that made it? He only recently contacted me. Old age has finally caught up to him. He's bee quite sick, and his dying wish is to see the pendant one last time. I didn't have the heart to tell him Tabitha lost it so many years ago. I'm ashamed to say I've been avoiding his calls." Jack explained. "It would be a wonderful opportunity to share it with him one last time, but it does belong to you now. The decision is yours."

Jen stood mesmerized by the sight of her necklace around the neck of a stranger. Mr. Johnson had to be telling the truth. There was no way that he would come up with a photo of his wife and such an intricate story at the drop of a hat. She had always wondered where Charli found the necklace, but never had the opportunity to ask. What were the odds of Jen reuniting with the pendant herself, but then the jewelry to be reunited with its very first owner and even its creator?

"Yes, I'd like that. I don't know why this little charm has

made such an incredible journey back to us, but we can't exclude the jeweler that brought it to life." Jen said, still staring at the reflection of the photo.

"My sentiments exactly," Jack said before picking up his phone and making arrangements to meet with Paul.

Jack and Jen arrived at Paul's quiet brownstone less than an hour later. They climbed the steps, and Jen rang the doorbell.

"Coming. I'll be there in a moment." A frail voice called from behind the door.

Jack and Jen waited patiently until finally, the door slowly opened, revealing a feeble older man and his walker.

"Paul, my goodness, it's good to see you. I'm sorry that you haven't been well." Jack said, placing his hand on top of Paul's. "This is Jen. She owns the pendant now. It's made quite a journey since I had it commissioned. May we come in?"

"Jack Johnson. I never thought I'd see you again, son. Yes, please come in. And this young lady is Jen, you said? I thought you were giving the necklace to your wife." Paul said with a smile as he turned and shuffled through the entryway, carting his walker and oxygen tank along behind him. Jen and Jack followed him, being sure to close the door behind them.

The entryway led into a small parlor room where Paul invited his guests to take a seat.

"Yes. I did give the necklace to my wife. I'm ashamed to say that Tabitha lost it many years ago. Jen acquired it at some point after, and only today arrived in my office. As soon as I saw it, I knew it was ours. I'm having trouble believing it, Paul. This charm is special. You didn't just give it time and attention; you gave it life." Jack explained.

Paul let out a hearty laugh and sat into a tired old recliner chair.

"You don't say? I knew that little imp would find it's way

back to me one way or another, but that is quite a story. Do you have it? Can I see it?."

Jen carefully unhooked the clasp from her wrist and passed the bracelet to Jack, who then passed it to Paul. As soon as the sterling touched Paul's frail, tired skin, the entire bracelet began to glow, and the front door of the house was thrown open in a fury of a mighty wind.

Paul laughed once again.

"Yes, yes. I'm glad to see you too. Stop that. You'll scare the neighbors." Paul scolded as he brought the necklace to his chest.

As suddenly as it began, the wind stopped, and the door quietly swung shut.

"That's better." Paul laughed.

Jack and Jen sat in complete awe. Each of them knew the charm possessed some magic after the happiness it brought to their lives. Witnessing the magic first hand was almost overwhelming.

"I know. It's something, isn't it? As soon as I began working on this piece, that wind and other unexplainable things began to follow me around." Paul explained. He noticed the dumbfounded expressions across each face sitting in front of him. "As soon as it left my shop, all the mystery and essence went with it. I've never believed in much outside of the physical realm, but this pendant gave me something to look forward to after death. It was one of my last commissions before I closed the shop. I've since invested my time in God, renewing my faith and making amends with my children. After their mother passed things were difficult between us and I never realized it. I was lost in my grief and mad at the Man Upstairs. You know how it goes, Jack."

Jack nodded in response. He did understand how grief and loss consumed people to the core of their souls. Grief had nearly killed Tabitha, until the necklace and it's magic intervened.

"Wow. That's amazing. I feel like a total idiot for ever letting it go." Jen exclaimed. She was speaking mostly to herself and thinking out loud.

"I'm familiar with Jack's story. What did it do for you, Ms. Jen?" Paul asked.

Jen looked at Paul's weathered face as she thought about what significance the pendant had brought to her life. As she thought, she remembered the night she ended the relationship with Nate, and a smile spread across her face.

"It gave me the strength to end the relationship with my abuser and propelled me forward into my new life. When my boyfriend's mom gave me the pendant, she told me that I deserved happiness, but I don't think I quite believed it until the moment I was sitting in on my bedroom floor crying after catching my boyfriend, her son, with another woman. I clung to it that night, hoping beyond hope that it would bring me happiness as I left everything I knew behind. It did." Jen explained.

Paul leaned forward in his chair and held out the bracelet to Jen.

"Here, Jen. I think this belongs to you now." Paul said as Jen reached out and accepted the bracelet. "Thank you for allowing me to hold this little slice of magic one more time. I hope it continues to bring you many more blessings. Jack, thank you for giving me the opportunity to find my faith again during these last years of my life. Although, I don't think the magic that surrounds this pendant comes from the silver and niello itself. No, this magic is something that comes from, well, I think it's present inside of all of us. Sometimes we just need a little bit of whimsy and sterling to bring it out."

ABOUT THE AUTHOR

Rebecca MacCeile is a loving wife and mom to three rambunctious kids, twin boys and a girl. She has been an avid blogger, blogging about her life and the challenges of marriage since 2011, motherhood since 2012, and the recovery process she went through after being diagnosed with PTSD in 2013.

When she's not writing, or spending time with her family she is a dedicated volunteer for A Voice for the Innocent. AVFTI is a wonderful organization dedicated to helping survivors of sexually based crimes share their stories and find local resources to offer a community of support.

For more information or to share your story please visit:

http://www.avoicefortheinnocent.org

ALSO BY REBECCA MACCEILE

Candy Apple Butterscotch: A Memoir
Novelties: A Collection of Unfinished Short Stories
Turquoise Boot Straps: A Survivor's Thoughts
Eleanor's Library

You can find the most up to date information about Rebecca and her upcoming projects at:

http://www.rebeccasbookshop.com

Made in the USA
Monee, IL
17 April 2021